POISONOUS CITY

POISONOUS CITY

Robert Jeffries

Copyright © 2023 Robert Jeffries.

No part of this publication may be reproduced, stored in a retrieval system, or transmitted in any form or by any means, electronic, mechanical, photocopying, recording, or otherwise, without written permission of the publisher.

This is a work of fiction. Names, characters, businesses, places, events, locales, and incidents are either the products of the author's imagination or used in a fictitious manner. Any resemblance to actual persons, living or dead, or actual events is purely coincidental.

All rights reserved including the right of reproduction in whole or in part in any form. The moral right of the author has been asserted.

This book is dedicated to my friends Isabel Sitz and Barry Needoff - your enthusiasm has been so important to me.
Thank you.

Foreword

The story that follows is a work of fiction set in a late nineteenth century London still trying to come to grips with the horrors that became known as 'The Whitechapel Murders'. However, amongst the fiction there are elements of truth and fact. Some of the events that I relate actually took place on the streets of London and some of the characters that appear in the story really did exist. I hope that the reader will derive some amusement and enjoyment in working out where truth becomes fiction and where fact dissolves into fantasy.

At the conclusion of the tale I will separate fact from fiction … I believe (and hope) that readers may well find some interesting surprises in the following pages.

Chapter One

Inspector Peter Randan of New Scotland Yard's Detective Branch emerged from the gloom of Westminster Underground Station into the brightness of a cool, sunny autumn morning in Central London. As usual he glanced up at the clock tower of the Houses of Parliament and checked his own pocket watch against it. He pulled out the winder and advanced the minute hand a little before applying four full rotations to the winding mechanism and replacing the watch back into his waistcoat pocket.

He walked along Bridge Street towards Parliament Square before turning right along Parliament Street and right again into Derby Gate. Passing through the open wrought iron gates, he walked into New Scotland Yard.

Entering the main building he climbed two flights of stairs and turned the handle of the door marked Criminal Records Office. Closing the door behind him he placed his brown derby hat on top of a wooden hat stand, removed his coat and jacket and placed them on wooden hangers.

In the small adjoining office next to his he could hear his assistant already busy at her work. "Good morning, Joan, how are you?"

"I'm fine thank you Mr. Randan, I've already placed a bundle of files on your desk for you to check. When you've amended them just bring them through to me and I will finish them up for you."

"Thank you, Joan. It looks as if we have yet another breathlessly exciting day ahead of us. Files, more files and ever more files for us to deal with."

"I know it's not what you want to be doing, sir, but I'm sure your promotion will come about soon and then you'll be back in the thick of the action again, even though I will be desperately sorry to see you leave."

"You're an angel, Joan, but you're an overly optimistic angel, I fear. The inspectors being promoted these days are those working out on division, the men making the arrests, the men carrying out the primary objectives of policing. They are the men being 'made up', not deskbound officers like myself who spend their time polishing leather seats in offices like this. It's very much a case of 'out of sight, out of mind' I'm afraid, and I think you will be stuck with me for some time yet."

"I'm sure your time will come, sir. In the meantime, I'll put the kettle on. I'm sure a nice cup of tea and one of my scones will make you feel better."

"What would I do without you, Joan? You make life here tolerable!"

"I'll bring them into you, sir."

Thirty minutes later Joan knocked on his door and entered just as Randan finished his scone. "There's a lady here to see you, Mr Randan."

"A lady?"

"Yes, sir – and I mean 'A Lady'. She says her name is Lady Valerie Meux. She's terribly elegant, has a very posh accent and is asking for you by name."

"Really? Can't say as the name rings any bells but I suppose you had better show her in."

A few seconds later, Joan showed the visitor into Randan's office "This is Lady Meux, sir."

Joan had not exaggerated. Lady Meux was tall, beautiful, and extremely elegant. Randan guessed she might be in her mid to late thirties and her clothes looked as if they had come directly from the Paris Spring collections.

"Joan, could you find us two more cups of tea and

perhaps one of your scones for her Ladyship?"

"Yes, sir, of course."

When Lady Meux spoke, her accent identified her as belonging to the very highest ranks of society. "Thank you for seeing me without an appointment Inspector Randan. It really is most kind of you."

"Not at all, your ladyship; how may I be of service?"

"You are being *very* formal Inspector. I suspect that you don't recognise me."

Randan looked confused. "I'm afraid you have me at a great disadvantage, your ladyship. I am sure I would have remembered if we had met before."

She smiled at him. "It was a long time ago and our circumstances were somewhat different in those days. You were a handsome young police officer and I – well, let's just say for now that I was certainly *not* Lady Meux. Perhaps if I remind you of the very first words you may have heard me speak on the occasion when we first met, that might jog your memory?"

"Possibly," replied Randan.

"I think I said something like" – and instantly her upper class Mayfair accent became one that you might hear more often on the Mile End Road – "This bloody copper has just saved my life! Now what the bleedin' 'ell were *you* bunch of clowns playing at while he was doing it? Bugger all! That's what!" She now smiled sweetly at Randan. "Now, do please close your mouth Peter. You look as if you are trying to catch flies."

Randan looked closely at her face for the first time. "Val? Valerie Susan Langdon? Is it really you?"

"As ever was Peter. It took a little time but I do believe the penny has finally dropped. It's been a while since we last saw each other and I am sincerely flattered that you can even remember my full name."

"A while? It must be thirteen or fourteen years at least and there are some things in life that one simply never forgets".

"Yes, indeed, so many years, Peter. Is it all right for me

to call you Peter? I would rather we were on first name terms."

Randan nodded his agreement "Of course, Lady ... I mean, Valerie."

"We've both come a long way since those days, Peter. Look at you! An inspector at New Scotland Yard!"

"And you have joined the aristocracy."

"I have, Peter and it is quite true to say that you played a part in that happy turn of events."

"Really? I find that hard to believe. We only met on one occasion."

"It really is quite true, I assure you."

Joan knocked twice and re-entered the office holding a tray with tea and a couple of scones on it. She was rather surprised to see both of them looking so relaxed. "I've put a little dish of butter on the side for your ladyship."

Once again Valerie's accent returned to the upper class version. "Thank you so much, Joan, this is really so kind of you to go to all this trouble."

Joan blushed at the compliment "Well, I suppose I'd better let you two get on."

"Thank you, Joan", said Randan "Will you hold any other visitors for the time being please?"

"There hasn't been another visitor here for you in the last two years, sir, but if they do appear outside, I shall ask them to form an orderly queue."

"Yes, thank you, Joan, that will be all for now!"

"Lady ... sorry, Valerie, I suspect that you haven't come here to chat about the old times?"

"Actually, Peter, that is exactly why I am here, at least, in a manner of speaking. Years ago when I really needed help you came to my aid and today I find that once again I am in need of police assistance and I'm afraid I don't know many police officers. Indeed, I don't know *any* other police officers so it seemed natural to me to seek out the one officer I know I can trust."

It was Randan's turn to smile "You are flattering me."

Valerie smiled sweetly. "Of course I am! Now, let's get

started. Peter, I want to take you back to when we first met. Trust me, there is a link to the main reason why I have come to see you here today. On that night when our paths first crossed at the Casino de Venice, I would like you to tell me how you would have described my role at the Casino?"

"In my report I described you as a barmaid at the Casino."

Val grinned. "You are polite and very discreet, Peter. I can see that I was right to seek your help. I may have started at the Casino as a barmaid, but by the time of the incident we are talking about, I was also working as a prostitute and you know that very well, so let's not beat about the bush. There is no need to spare my blushes, I left those far behind me many years ago. Now, tell me what you remember of that night."

"It was a Friday evening I believe. I was a young constable working late-turn at Holborn Police Station. At about nine I was walking past the Casino de Venice when a young lady came running out shouting that one of her friends was being assaulted inside. I followed her upstairs to find a small group of your colleagues trying to open the door. They told me that it had been locked from the inside and they couldn't open it, so I took a run up and put my shoulder to the door. Fortunately, it was enough to break the lock. I seem to recall that I rather fell into your room. Inside, I saw a man with his hands around your throat and you were … erm … wearing considerably less than you are wearing now."

Val interrupted his narrative. "Now, let me explain how I came to be employed at the Casino de Venice."

"Let me stop you there," Randan interjected. "Whatever happened that night and whatever your terms of employment at the Casino de Venice may have been, they are of no importance to me now; you owe me nor anyone else for that matter any sort of explanation for what happened fourteen or so years ago. If you require police assistance now, you are absolutely entitled to it and your past history is irrelevant"

Again she smiled and reached across the desk to touch his hand. "Peter, please allow me to do this in my own way.

Shortly I will give you some information which I suppose you might describe as 'Criminal Intelligence' but before I impart that information to you I need you to understand exactly how I came to be in possession of this information and to do that, you need to know the full story. But I fully intend to enjoy Joan's tea and scones while I am telling the story."

Having taken a sip of her tea, she began. "I was born and grew up in Devon but as my father was a butcher I was never going to go into the family business and I never really did feel that I wanted to live my life in Devon, so, aged twenty three I decided to make my way to London. I didn't have any money so I walked or begged rides in carts and wagons and slept wherever I could find somewhere dry and safe. When I got to a new town or village I would try and find some work, usually in taverns or inns where the landlord knew that a new and pretty young girl behind the bar brought in paying customers. It took me over two months to get there but eventually I arrived in London and again I looked for work in shops or wherever I could, but the work I enjoyed most was behind the bar in various pubs. One day I was working in a pub not far from Lincoln's Inn when I noticed a man paying me particular attention. Eventually, he told me he was the owner of the Casino de Venice and that he could always find work for a good barmaid. I told him that I was quite happy where I was, but he said that whatever wages I was getting at the pub, he would double if I went to work for him. I told him that I would need to see the place first before making a decision and he told me to come and see him the next day and he would show me around. So the next day I went to the Casino. As soon as I saw all the girls hanging around the bar area I knew exactly what sort of place it was. I may have been a bit naive but I wasn't stupid, neither was I a virgin but I certainly had no intentions of working as a whore in the Casino de Venice and I told him that straight out. He said that was all right and that I could just work behind the bar if that's what I wanted. For the first couple of months it all worked quite well and I found that I fitted in without any problem, but although the money was better than I got working in ordinary pubs, it was obvious that the 'Upstairs Girls' were all earning quite a lot more than me. I started to think that, if I was going out with some of the men that I met in the bar, what would be so wrong in me getting paid properly for doing exactly the same as I was already doing for free? So I had a word with the owner and told him that I might be prepared to become an 'Upstairs Girl'. Most of the girls thought I was being sensible but I know for a fact that some of them had their noses put severely out of joint because I proved to be very good at the work and before long I proved to be the most popular girl at the Casino. By now it was 1875 and I'd been in London for about two years; the incident which you became involved in happened the following year. The man was just another client. We chatted for a while in the bar and we had a couple of drinks before I agreed to go upstairs with him. He must have had some drink before coming to the Casino because I quickly realised that he would have trouble performing. I didn't have a set time for clients but when I realised that he had nodded off to sleep and was actually snoring, I decided that his time was well and truly up. Most similar establishments have a set of rules for dealing with 'problem' clients. At the Casino, each room had a push bell system for warning the other staff when any of the girls had a problem. I reached across to ring the bell but in doing so I woke the man up. He must have realised what I was doing and he suddenly became aggressive. At first we were struggling with each other for what seemed like an eternity then he suddenly started to hit me. I screamed and screamed for help and made towards the door but he grabbed me from behind and began to throttle me. I began to black out and I can remember staring at the door and thinking to myself that that door was probably the last thing that I would ever see. Then, you suddenly crashed through the door and the man turned his attention to you. I think you tried to wrestle him out but he was punching you and I seem to recall you suffered a black eye in the exchange? Anyway, you changed your tactics and delivered what I believe in the world of prize fighting would be described as a 'crisp right hook' which sent him back to sleep. And I launched into my tirade against the men who were being paid to keep us girls safe. At that point I thought you would cart him off to the police station and that would be an end to it, but no. You had already probably saved my life but you then greatly surprised me. You completely ignored my attacker, instead you took my dressing gown from the hook and covered what little remaining modesty I had. You then insisted on personally treating my wounds."

Randan broke in. "You did have a very nasty gash above your left eye that I could see would need stitching and I needed to apply direct pressure to the wound to staunch the bleeding."

"I still have the scar, Peter and if it hadn't been for you, my scar would have been a lot more visible than it is. Also, you insisted that a doctor be summoned immediately to tend to me. Then you left and I had no expectation of seeing you again, until a couple of days later one of the other girls at the Casino informed me that you had called around asking to speak to me again."

"Yes, the owner said he was unwilling to press charges and I wanted to try and persuade you to press charges yourself."

"I know that, but we both now know that was never going to be allowed to happen; it would mean too much bad publicity for the place. I was told by the owner that the occasional beating was an 'occupational hazard' for girls in my line of work, but he also told me something else. He told me that the *real* reason for you coming back to speak to me was so that you could 'claim your reward' for helping me. He said it happened all the time and that he had done me a favour by sending you away."

Randan visibly bristled at the suggestion, even all those years later. "That is simply not true Valerie. He was lying to you!"

"Calm down Peter. I now know that was not the case, though I must admit it made sense to me at the time. But then one of the other girls at the Casino told me the truth the following day; she said that she had spoken to you away from the owner and that she was convinced of your honest intentions. 'After all,' she said, 'If he couldn't claim his reward from you, why wouldn't he claim it from me instead?' And so my good feelings regarding your kind intentions were restored and have remained with me ever since. Indeed, that incident and the part you played in it changed my life. I suddenly realised that remaining at the Casino de Venice might well see me ending my days in either the poor house, the mad house or the mortuary, possibly even all three. So I began to think of ways out. I thought about the possibility of perhaps going into entertainment and starting a career in the theatre and if it was just a few years later then I suppose I might have been a Gaiety Girl – but that was not to be. Fortunately, although I couldn't possibly have known it at the time, my whole world was about to change and within a few months my time at the Casino de Venice would be well and truly behind me."

"May I ask how that happened?" Randan enquired.

"Why, I met my husband, of course, Peter."

"And he is?"

"Oh, I'm so sorry, Peter, I should have told you. He is Henry Bruce Meux, the third Baronet of Theobalds Park. They are one of the richest families in the country, having made their fortune in the brewing industry."

"I see, I didn't realise that, Val. One question does occur to me, however, and please excuse me if you consider this question to be impertinent. Does your husband, Henry, wasn't it? Does he know about your time at the Casino de Venice?"

"Peter, I thought you were a detective! *Of course* he knows about my time at the Casino! Where on earth do you think we met? Do you imagine that perhaps I invited myself to tea with Henry and his family at Theobalds Park? No, of course not! I met him when he was a client of mine at the Casino! By the way – I must ask Joan for the recipe for her scones; they really are most awfully delicious and I would very much like to be able to pass it onto my pastry chef."

Randan gazed at Valerie across his desk. "So, you are telling me that you met your future husband, Henry, a prominent member of the British aristocracy when he was a client of yours at the Casino de Venice?"

"Exactly, Peter. Is it really so hard to believe?"

"Let's just say that it is not the scenario that I would imagine might precede most successful marriages."

"Well, we are all different. Wouldn't the world be a duller place if we always lived our lives as convention demands?"

"I can't argue with that."

"My life has contained a great many sins, Peter, but I can promise you that *all* my sins – well most of them, anyway – occurred before I met Henry and since I became his wife I have led an exemplary lifestyle, not that most of Henry's family will believe that to be the case. As far as they are concerned, I am the Devil incarnate. A sorceress who has bewitched poor Henry and now holds him, and his money, in my thrall".

"So, the Casino de Venice is a dark and distant thing from your past?"

"Absolutely. Nothing exists from that period of my life except memories."

Randan couldn't resist a smirk as he looked at her over his steepled fingers "What – not even your banjo playing?"

"How in God's name do you know about that?" She giggled.

"Your colleague mentioned it to me when I returned to the Casino after your assault."

"Did she mention anything else about me?"

"Not really, only that you were mostly well liked by the other girls and that the owner saw you as a prized asset that he would do pretty much anything to keep at the Casino. And I have to say, it is also one of the main reasons why the name Valerie Susan Langdon has lingered so long in my memory. It really is quite difficult to forget the image of a banjo playing prostitute."

"Well, when you put it like that, I suppose it must be

and for your information, yes, I do still play the banjo, but only for Henry. And for the zebras, I suppose; they seem to quite enjoy the sound and for some reason it seems to relax them."

"Did you just say zebras?"

"Yes. I have two stables where I keep zebras. I keep several in a mews stable near Hyde Park but my four favourite zebras I keep mostly in my stables at Theobalds Park. Jacob, Joshua, Isabel and little Percy, he's my latest addition to the stables. I use them to pull my carriage around the estate and when I visit the local towns; the local children love them so. And when you see the look on the faces of the people of London when you drive past them in a carriage pulled by zebras – well, let us just say that it creates an impression"

"Of course it would. How stupid of me!"

"I enjoy being unconventional, Peter. Would you like to hear how Henry and I first met?"

"You have already told me that he was a client at the Casino. Do I need to know anything more?"

"Oh don't be such a 'fuddy-duddy' Peter! There really is great deal more to the story than simply that. And some might even consider our story as a true romance. Also, it's a story which only Henry and I know about, so I am simply dying to tell it to someone else."

"In that case, please proceed."

"After my assault, I quickly realised that I needed to leave the Casino lifestyle behind me. I examined various options and I thought that perhaps I could make a life for myself in the theatre. However, I swiftly realised that opportunities for banjo playing prostitutes in the legitimate theatre were fairly few and far between but I resigned myself to keep on searching for a way out of the Casino. As you are already aware, the owner was intent on keeping me at the Casino and he was quite generous towards me with financial inducements. One day he called me to his office, gave me an envelope and told me to go out and buy something 'fetching'. I didn't need persuading and I went straight to Piccadilly. I spent some time window shopping and went into a ladies' outfitters with a French name and asked the assistant to show me what they had. She looked at me as if I was something nasty that she had just trodden in and said, 'I'm afraid that this establishment may well be out of Madame's price range,' at which I simply took out my envelope, removed the banknotes, dropped them on the counter and looked at her – rather like you are looking at me right now, Peter, sort of sideways. Anyway, her attitude rapidly changed and eventually I selected a gorgeous dress, classy but revealing in all the right places, if you get my drift. After I had tried it on to make sure that it fitted me perfectly, she wrapped it up, put it in a fancy bag and I took it back to the Casino. I went upstairs to put my new dress on and when the Casino opened for business, I made my grand entrance. Of course, everybody admired the dress and I was loving the attention. At about seven in the evening, four young gentlemen entered the club. They were obviously very well to do and the owner was plainly expecting them. He got them a drink and they were deep in conversation for some time then after a while he waved me over and told me that the young gentlemen would be holding a birthday celebration for one of their close friends who would be arriving shortly and that he wanted me to host the event, It was the occasion of their friend's eighteenth birthday and they believed it was high time that he should take his first steps into adulthood. Suddenly, I realised why I had been given the money to buy the dress that afternoon and from the look on those lads faces it was clearly making the impression that the owner had hoped for. The young men said that their friend's name was Henry and they said that he was rather shy. The owner told them not to worry as there was nobody in London better placed to make Henry's birthday a memorable occasion than 'our Valerie'."

Again Randan interjected. "As I said, Valerie, what is in the past is not really relevant and I don't think you need to tell me the full details of your first encounter with Henry."

Valerie grinned broadly. "Come along, Peter. You really should be getting the hang of this by now. With me, you should always expect the unexpected. I have no intention of revealing any salacious details for the very simple reason there are no such details to reveal. Now, if I may be allowed to continue? A little while later Henry arrived with another of his friends and we all sat down with some champagne. I later found out that poor Henry had absolutely no idea what his chums had planned for him and although he was, shall we say 'inexperienced' he wasn't stupid and as soon as he saw the type of place that the Casino was he realised what his friends had arranged and his sense of security was most definitely not strengthened by the sight of me wearing *that* dress. But, bless his heart, he kept smiling through what must have been an awful ordeal. Shortly, after a couple of glasses of bubbly, I whispered in his ear that I had a birthday present waiting for him upstairs and I took his hand and led him upstairs to the VIP suite. As we climbed the stairs I could almost feel his nervousness, he was actually trembling but he simply was not going to let his friends down. When we were out of sight of the main salon, I stopped him and asked him if he was feeling alright. He said he was. I asked him if he had ever been to a place like the Casino before and he assured me that he had not. Then I asked him the vital question, although I already knew what his answer would be. I asked him if he had ever been with a woman before? And he confirmed, rather sheepishly, that this was his first time alone with a woman. I told him not to worry and that he did not have to do anything that he did not want to do. He told me that it was unthinkable for him to back out of what his friends had planned so I took him into the room and closed the door behind us. The poor boy was completely petrified so I poured him a glass of water, sat next to him on the bed and we just talked. I told him that places like the Casino existed for a reason but that they were really not the ideal place for a handsome young man to gain his very first amorous experience. I told him that his friends thought they were doing him a favour, but that paying a woman like me to give him his first taste of sensuality was far from being the ideal and that in years to come, when he met someone that he *really* loved, this memory could prove to be a real embarrassment. But, bless him, he hated the idea of letting his chums down. So I told him that they need never know. In a couple of hours time we could go back to the salon, he could thank them for their generosity and if they asked me what he was like, I would tell them that he was an absolute stallion and that I was now quite exhausted. Then they could all get drunk in celebration and nobody would ever be any the wiser. And that is exactly what happened – nothing! We had a couple more glasses of champagne each and we chatted about his life and his hopes and a couple of hours later I took him back to his friends. After a few more drinks they all left having settled their rather large bill with the owner and I thought I would never see young Henry again – but I was wrong. About a month later I was in the salon at the Casino. It was just after opening time and things were very quiet. I was chatting to one of the other girls with my back to the front door. Suddenly the girl I was chatting with asked me if the young man she had just seen enter the salon wasn't the same young gentleman with whom I had celebrated his eighteenth birthday a few weeks before? I turned around and sure enough Henry had come in all on his own. I went across to him and asked him if he was all right and he just gave me a nervous smile and asked if there was somewhere private where we could chat. Normally the owner would frown on such a thing, he wanted guests to be entertained in the bar area where they would have to be drinking, but as I knew the owner was out on other business, I ushered Henry into a back office and asked him what he wanted. He told me that he very much appreciated the way I had handled the situation when he and his friends had last visited the Casino but now he had time to reflect on his position and he realised that it really *was* time that he had his first amorous adventure and he would very much like it to be with me, providing I didn't mind of course. I have to tell you, Peter, that my heart just melted for him. He just looked so sweet and so completely out of place in that den of iniquity, but I knew that for his own sake I had to be firm with him! I told him that I was deeply flattered by his intentions, however none of what he said altered in any way the fact that a handsome young man in his social position should not be paying to lose his virginity in a brothel. He looked so disappointed and I realised that he must have been building up the courage to come back to the Casino for ages and I felt awful in turning him down. But I knew I was right; then I had an idea. I told him that I would make a bargain with him. He must leave the Casino before the owner returned. He must then wait for at least another month to pass and if he still felt the same way about me then he could return to the Casino and bring with him a small posy of flowers with a card that said 'To Valerie, Sincerest regards, Henry'. Clients often brought in such tributes for the girls and the owner encouraged the practice as it encouraged clients to frequent the club on a more regular basis. This gesture would act as a signal between us, and I would know that he still wanted us to meet together. I would then attend a hotel of his choice five nights later at seven in the evening. This would all mean that Henry would get his wish but at least our meeting would be between two fully consenting adults and at least he would not be paying for the privilege in the Casino de Venice. He suggested the Andover Hotel in Gower Street and we sealed the agreement with a single kiss before he left. The other girl asked what he had wanted and I told her that after he and his friends had left the Casino after their last visit they had all gone off and got drunk. When he woke up next morning he realised that he had lost a set of keys during the celebrations and he wondered if perhaps he had left them here. She told me that it was a good job that he didn't lose his wallet as he might be accusing me of robbing him! I don't mind telling you Peter that my feelings were torn. Part of me was hoping that Henry would come to his senses and that I would never see or hear from him again, but another part of me wanted him to bring that posy."

"And I am guessing that he did?" enquired Randan

"Yes, Peter. Indeed he did. He followed my instructions to the letter and exactly one month later I was informed that a young gentleman admirer had left his card with a posy of flowers. Of course, the owner was delighted as he thought that would mean that Henry and possibly his friends would once again be visiting the Casino."

"One question, Valerie; why did you stipulate that you would meet him five nights after he delivered his posy?"

"Meeting clients away from the Casino was strictly against house rules and therefore forbidden. The owner would have been furious with me if he knew what I was doing and a five night break between receiving the posy and actually meeting Henry was just sufficient for me to arrange time off from the Casino and not arouse any suspicions. I told the owner that I would need to take a few days off as I had received notice that my mother was unwell back in Devon and that I would have to return home. He wasn't happy but I stood firm and he agreed I could have some time off."

"Very clever, I must say. And the meeting was a success?"

"Oh yes, Peter. Our planned one night assignation turned into three nights that I can't even begin to describe to you. It was simply magical and not *just* in the way that you are plainly imagining from the smirk on your face, although that part of it *was* very good too, I must say."

"I do apologise, Valerie. I did not mean my expression to be so obvious."

"I forgive you, Peter. We ate at wonderful restaurants, went to the theatre to see real plays and not just music hall acts. Everything was perfect and I was loving the whole experience, until the last morning. Then it all went wrong."

Chapter Two

"What exactly went wrong?" Randan enquired.

"Everything! I had planned the whole thing so carefully. My intention was to get Henry over his youthful infatuation with me and once that had been achieved we would both go our separate ways and never see each other again. He would take his place in polite society and I would go back to my life, such as it was. But I failed to take into account one very important thing."

"And that was?"

"In all of his life, nobody had ever explained to Henry what the word 'no' meant. It was a word that he simply didn't understand."

"And why did that spoil all your plans?"

"We woke up after our third night together. He had already told me the previous night that he had some important business to attend to that day and I decided that this morning would be the perfect time to kiss him farewell, which is what I did. He just looked at me strangely and asked me what I meant by 'Farewell'? I told him that I had had a wonderful time and that I would never forget his kindness and generosity but that he must get back to his life, just as I must get back to mine. He just shook his head and told me that I could not be serious. He kept asking why on earth would I want to go back to that awful place? I tried to explain that we all have to make our way through life as best we can, he by running his business and me at the Casino, though I was working on ways of putting my old life behind me and moving on to something better. He then told me that this was an excellent idea and that I should let him help me with that plan. I just smiled and asked him how he intended to do that? Perhaps by offering me employment at Theobalds Park? Because I knew that would never work, to which he then told me that the only position he was prepared to offer me was that of being his wife and that he thought I would make an excellent Lady Meux! I burst out laughing at the foolishness of what he had just said and asked him if he had lost his mind? Such a thing was simply not possible. I told him that his family would never stand for him marrying beneath his social rank. They would disinherit him. But everything I said he had an answer for. They could not disinherit him because he was already legally the third Baronet of Theobalds Park. He could do whatever he liked. So I decided to employ shock tactics. I laid everything out plainly before him and I reminded him that he was an aristocrat and that I was a whore who sold my body in a brothel. It would be simply unthinkable for us to be man and wife. Do you know what he said to that?"

"No, but I imagine you are about to tell me."

"He told me that we were now living in the 1870s and that things had moved on in this modern age. The world and even the English class system was changing. Lots of men who he knew had married women of a different social status and they had all managed to survive – well, mostly. I really didn't know what to think so I insisted that I had to get back to the Casino. I needed some time to think. He held me in his arms and told me that he meant every word he had said and that his mind was made up. He told me that I should go back to the Casino for as long as it would take me to hand in my notice. He simply could not live with the thought of me being with other men and from that moment on I could feel my control of everything just slipping away so I didn't answer him. Then he kissed me and he made me promise him that I would let him take me away from 'that awful place'. I nodded and tried to get away to let my mind settle. Then he said it!"

"Said what, Valerie?"

"He told me that he loved me and I just stood there crying. It felt as if I had been kicked in the stomach. I had no idea why I was crying, but I was. I hugged him and kissed him goodbye. We agreed to meet for lunch at the Savoy Grill at two in the afternoon to finalise our plans – or, rather, his plans! I couldn't get away fast enough. I went to my lodgings and fortunately my friend Rose was there. She is the lady you chatted to after the assault - Rose and I were very close, we still are as a matter of fact. We trusted each other with all our secrets. She knew where I had been for the last few days and when I told her what had happened, she threw her arms around me and told me that my life was never going to be the same ever again. I told her that she was as mad as Henry and that I could *never* be his wife. She took me by the shoulders and told me that I was the mad one, that this was my big and possibly only chance to leave my old life behind me and that I should just grab it with both hands and offer thanks to whatever guardian angel happened to be looking after me on the day I met the third Baronet Henry Bruce Meux."

"Rose sounds like an eminently sensible person."

"She is, and for the very first time I actually began to wonder whether Henry and I might actually have a future together. I told Rose that I was meeting Henry at the Savoy Grill for lunch and she helped me to get ready then I took a slow walk to the Victoria Embankment in order to clear my mind. I arrived just before two and Henry was standing in Embankment Gardens close to the entrance to the Savoy Grill. I asked him how on earth he was going to smuggle me past the Maitre d'? Henry laughed and whispered that he had no intention of smuggling me anywhere and he would simply introduce me to Joseph and he promised I would like him. He told me that once he had informed Joseph that I was a very dear friend of his then I would be free to come and go whenever I pleased and he assured me that the Savoy Grill would *never* be closed to me. Oh, how I longed to believe him, Peter, but I just couldn't bring myself to actually believe.

When we entered, Joseph just seemed to appear out of thin air and Henry introduced me. Joseph simply smiled, bowed his head towards me and said that he was charmed and honoured to meet me. I wondered what he would think If only he knew the truth. I think Henry could read my thoughts and he whispered that as far as Joseph was concerned, there is no such thing as right or wrong, good or bad. There is merely discretion and Joseph is known throughout the civilised world as the very soul of discretion. As we drank our glasses of champagne, Henry told me that he had done a great deal of thinking and wanted to discuss some ideas with me. I told him that I was deeply flattered but that he must put these foolish ideas from his mind. As usual he just ignored my protestations. He begged me to just listen to what he had to say. He wanted me to resign from the Casino de Venice with immediate effect, that night if possible, the sooner I was out of there the happier he would be. He said that he would find me appropriate furnished accommodation and he would ensure I had sufficient credit to obtain a suitable wardrobe. I really did think that I was in some sort of fantasy. Then he looked at me very intently and told me that he had also given a great deal of thought to what I had said earlier, about me never being accepted into society and he told me that we must invent some kind of cover story, perhaps based on my thoughts that I could escape from the Casino by becoming a legitimate actress?"

"That could work I suppose," offered Randan.

"I doubted that it would work in fact but I found myself agreeing to give it a try. Henry told me to choose a stage name. I did not have a clue what he was talking about but he told me that every actor or actress had a stage name. I gave it some thought and came up with Val Reece. I used to know a girl called Val Reece back in Devon and I didn't think she would mind me borrowing her name. Henry agreed with me and laid out his ideas. Henry loved going to the theatre and on one visit he saw Val Reece on stage and was immediately struck by her beauty and her talent. He waited outside the stage door at the end of her performance and presented her with a bunch of flowers. Henry and Val met on several occasions and eventually fell in love with each other. I said that being an actress was (I supposed) a much more acceptable career to polite society than being a prostitute."

"Even a banjo playing prostitute?" queried the detective with a smirk.

"Don't be smutty, Peter but yes, far more suitable – or so I thought. But Henry had other ideas too. His last suggestion was perhaps the cleverest. He wanted me to go to a 'finishing school' so I could be taught how to be a 'Lady'."

"Really?"

"Yes, absolutely, and it was a stroke of absolute genius, The lady he chose to be my teacher was one of his old tutors and she was devoted to him. She would do absolutely anything for him and she taught me all that she thought I needed to know about everything from fashion to etiquette. She even gave me elocution lessons. She is the reason why you failed to recognise me when I first entered your office."

"She certainly did a thorough job. Did you come up with any ideas yourself?"

"I did. Right at the end of lunch I suggested to Henry that if I was going to be moving to new accommodation and taking on all this re-education, it would be good for me to have some company. Henry considered this to be a very good idea and decided straight away that he would need to hire a lady's maid for me. I stopped him and said rather firmly that I did not want a maid but rather a companion and there was no need to hire anyone because I knew exactly who my companion should be. It simply had to be Rose. If I was going to escape from the Casino, I had to bring her with me. I could not live with myself knowing that I had escaped and left her behind. Henry just laughed and agreed."

"So, it was as simple as that?"

"Yes, pretty much, Peter. But I then had to go and explain it all to Rose."

"Was she broadly in agreement?"

"You are joking, of course? She immediately burst into tears and then asked if she would have to curtsy every time I entered the room. I threatened to kick her down the nearest flight of stairs if she ever so much as thought of doing such a thing."

Peter steepled his fingers again "So you both left the Casino together? How did that go?"

"Actually, it was far easier than either of us expected. We decided to both go in together and simply tell the owner that we were leaving. We thought that being together would give us both a combined strength. I thought that he would try and place obstacles in our paths, after all, we were two of the most popular hostesses but he didn't; he simply said that if our plans didn't work out, then we could always apply to come back. In the circumstances I thought it best just to leave so we said goodbye to the other girls and walked away."

"It seems strange that he didn't even try to retain two of his main assets."

"I have thought about it quite often over the years and the answer I arrived at was simply that there were plenty of other girls like me and Rose in London. The truth is that he could probably walk into any gin palace and select a couple of pretty girls to replace us. Plus they would be younger than us and youth and beauty sells, Peter."

"Once you had left the Casino you must have still had your doubts? When was the first time you realised that this revolution in your life might actually work?"

"That's an easy question to answer. Rose and I both moved into our new accommodation, a beautifully comfortable apartment just off Berkeley Square in Mayfair. I decided to put our new lifestyle to an immediate test. I told Rose to put on something suitable as we were going out for lunch. We stepped out into Berkeley Square and I hailed a hansom cab and told the cabbie to take us to the Savoy Grill. Ten minutes later we drew up outside the Savoy. Rose was not at all sure about my idea and said as much. I repeated to her what Henry had told me about Joseph, the Maitre d', that once he knew I was a personal friend of his, then the Savoy Grill would never be closed to me. So, rather nervously, we agreed to put that promise to the test. When we entered through the River Terrace doors, I must admit that I was more than a little nervous. Perhaps we would be told that we must have an advance booking. Perhaps they would threaten to call the police to eject a couple of whores."

Randan looked quizzically across the desk "And ...?"

"Joseph appeared, as usual, from out of nowhere and welcomed us back to the Savoy Grill as if we were his oldest and dearest friends. Then he added that he had hoped he would have the pleasure of seeing me back again sooner rather than later. We followed him to Henry's favourite booth and that was the moment I knew that our lives had really changed for the better."

Randan smiled across his desk. "I'm sure that came as a great relief to you, but it is still a long way from being able to eat at the Savoy Grill to becoming Lady Valerie Meux, wife of one of the richest men in the country."

"Indeed, it is a long way, Peter, and believe me, nobody was more aware of that fact than myself. Not a day went by without me wondering if this would be the day when Henry finally came to his senses and realised that he had made a terrible mistake in getting involved with me! I even had an exit plan worked out in my mind for if and when that day finally arrived. My plan was to bow out with as much grace as a woman in my position could muster, then use my newly acquired skills in etiquette and elocution to try and find myself employment in a smart London shop."

"It's a good job that your future husband had other ideas, then."

"As I said earlier, nobody had ever taught dear Henry the meaning of the word 'No' and that, alongside the fact that he is one of this world's most obstinate men, really did work very much in my favour. Henry had decided that we were destined to be together, and nothing was going to get in the way of that happening."

"So how did you become Lady Valerie Meux? Was it a long engagement?"

"On the contrary, Peter, there was no engagement whatsoever. It all happened almost exactly three months after

Rose and I had left the Casino. I was with my tutor and Henry joined us. He asked my tutor how my lessons were progressing and she replied that in her opinion she had taught me all she could, to which Henry simply stated that he thought the time had come. I asked him what the time had come for? He replied very matter of factly that the time had come for us to be wed of course; what else could he be talking about?"

"A church wedding?"

"Good lord, no. That would have attracted far too much attention and would have ruined Henry's plans, such as they were. He told me to prepare myself to become Lady Meux the following Wednesday afternoon at two. He had chosen Westminster Town Hall in Caxton Street, Westminster. There would be just four of us at the ceremony, Henry and me plus our two witnesses who were to be Rose and my tutor, Eleanor. By two thirty we were leaving the office as Henry and Valerie Meux."

"As simple as that?"

"Absolutely. Mind you, that was the easy part! Henry then decided that our first official act as a wedded couple would be to go to his house or rather our house, I suppose I should say, where he would introduce me to his mother, the dowager Lady Meux."

"I see, and she knew nothing about the wedding?"

"Precisely. And not only did she know nothing about the wedding, she had no idea of my existence."

Peter arched his eyebrows. "I'm just guessing, but I somehow doubt if your first meeting with the other Lady Meux was a complete and unqualified success?"

"And you would be correct in that assumption. We arrived at Theobalds Park in the early evening and Henry guided me to the main withdrawing room where his mother was taking tea. I followed Henry into the room and he wished his mother a good afternoon and informed her that he had brought someone to meet her. He then introduced me as Lady Valerie Meux and explained to her that I had graciously accepted his proposal of marriage and that we had become husband and wife that very afternoon. There was a short silence and his mother asked if he was playing some kind of foolish joke? Henry then took my hand as he explained to his mother that this was certainly not a joke and that I had made him the happiest man in all the world."

"How did his mother take this news?"

"I think it would be fair to say that she was not desperately happy for us but it was difficult to gauge her exact thoughts because she displayed not one tiny sign of emotion. She just stared at me for a full ten seconds and then spoke very quietly and with great authority as she told Henry to leave us immediately. He made to object but she cut him short and she repeated her order telling him that what she and I were going to say to each other was none of his business. I flashed a small smile to Henry and asked him to do as his mother had asked and Henry reluctantly left the room and closed the door behind him. His mother remained completely still and just stared at me. Then she walked slowly around me but never took her eyes off of me for even a fraction of a second. I could see that she was a powerful and commanding woman. At last she spoke to me in a very calm voice, devoid of any emotion. 'My son called you Valerie? Well, Valerie, you are to be congratulated! I have no idea how you managed it but you would appear to have pulled off the coup of the century in persuading Henry to marry you. A quite remarkable feat I must say. However, I think we are both aware that this is all about money, isn't it? You must realise that it is one thing to marry Henry but entirely another thing to live the life of being Lady Meux. Along with the wealth comes enormous responsibility and in recognition of your magnificent effort I am going to make you a most generous offer. I will arrange for you to receive from my own personal funds the sum of £10,000 per annum for the rest of your natural life. This will mean that you will be able to live your life in style and comfort and without suffering the least inconvenience caused by social responsibility. In return for this you will undertake never to see Henry again and not to place any impediment in the way of the divorce which I will obtain for you both. If you renege on this agreement then I will consider it null and void and you will be left penniless. Do we have an agreement?' It was my turn to stare at her for a good few seconds. I explained very calmly but with a smile on my face that if it was simply 'all about money' then I was afraid that a mere £10,000 per annum would not be a sum that I might even choose to consider as being sufficient compensation for my disappointing and deserting my poor Henry, whom I love most dearly. At last Her Ladyship broke into a grin of triumph. She said that she knew it! This was most certainly *all* about the money. She told me that I was definitely after a payoff and now we were merely haggling over my price! How much did I want per annum? £15,000? £20,000? I told her that, alas, she was mistaken. This really was nothing whatsoever to do with money. I simply wanted to see how much she was prepared to offer. The truth was that not even a million pounds per annum would persuade me to go against and betray Henry's love for me. I told her to keep her money and that I would continue to be Henry's lawful and loving wife for as long as he wanted me to remain so."

Randan gazed at Valerie with a look of true admiration "Bravo, Valerie. Well done, indeed. What did she say to that?"

"To me, nothing. She walked to the door and left the room. As she swept past Henry she told him that she would be leaving Theobalds Park immediately for her own estate and would not be returning. She told Henry that he might visit her whenever he pleased but that I would never be admitted."

"And were you and Henry's mother ever reconciled?"

"No, and I doubt we ever will be."

"I see," said Randan. "And so you became the one and only Lady Meux of Theobalds Park. That really is quite a story. But what it doesn't do however is explain your presence at New Scotland Yard today. Or, for that matter, how and why you tracked me down to this office."

"Ah yes. I do have a slight confession to make at this point. Earlier I told you that you were the only police officer that I have ever met. That is not strictly true. I do know one other Metropolitan Police officer."

"I see – and am I acquainted with him?"

"Yes, I imagine so. His name is Teddy Bradford."

"Do you mean Sir Edward Bradford? The newly appointed Commissioner of Police for the Metropolis?"

"Yes, of course. That's him. Teddy is a dear friend of Henry and myself and he has often joined us in Scotland at our hunting lodge. We have known him for many years. He had a distinguished military career before being appointed Commissioner of the Metropolitan Police, you know? When I realised that I was again in need of police assistance, I decided to ask Teddy if he knew you or could possibly find out if you were still actually a serving police officer. A few days ago Teddy sent me a message to say that you are indeed still in the police and also where I might be able to find you; and here I am."

Robert Jeffries

CHAPTER THREE

"Alright Valerie, now I know how you found me, but I remain none the wiser about why you have gone to so much trouble to find me."

"I have already told you, Peter! Please do try and pay attention! I find myself once again in need of police assistance, so surely it is only natural that I should seek out the man who has served me so well in the past?"

"Yes, but that last occasion was fourteen years ago and we are now both very different people. Tell me, Valerie, why exactly is it that you feel you need my assistance? There are a great many police officers in the Metropolitan Police Force and it may well be that one of them may be better able to assist you."

"Not so, Peter. This work will require not only your detective skills but also the utmost discretion. *That* is why I have come to you. But please don't rush me, Peter. Before I reveal all, I need to finish my story. Don't worry, I won't take up your whole day."

Peter opened his hands in a signal for her to continue.

"When I married Henry, of course I knew that he was a wealthy man, but I honestly didn't realise just how wealthy he actually was. Henry is one of the richest men in the whole country. His wealth is staggering. Obviously, as his wife, his wealth is my wealth! From the beginning he told me to do whatever I wanted, buy whatever I liked. I told him I might become an eccentric heiress. Do you know what he said? He told me that he was very happy for me to become an eccentric heiress. As long as I was the *most* eccentric heiress in the whole world. And that was a challenge that I was happy to accept. As far as most people in this country are aware, Lady Valerie Meux is a wasteful and wanton woman who has taken full advantage of her husband's vast wealth and will probably lead him to the very brink of bankruptcy. They firmly believe that my eccentricities will probably lead Henry directly to Carey Street."

"You don't seem overly concerned about what the rest of the world thinks about you, Valerie."

"You're absolutely correct, Peter. I don't care a fig about what the world thinks about me, because I know the truth. I very quickly realised that reckless spending was mind numbingly boring so I spoke to Henry and I asked him if he would object to me spending his money in ways that might benefit other people. He pointed out that there were a great many charities that already existed to help people in distressed circumstances and that is of course entirely true but I wanted to work along different lines. Charities have to work to a strict set of rules and I didn't want that. I wanted to spend our money in a way that I knew would benefit the people that I wanted to help."

"That sounds most philanthropic. How did you decide what to do and whom to help?"

"Rose and I sat down for lunch at the Savoy Grill and we both decided that the first people we should help were the women in London who had not had the benefit of our good fortune. We decided to seek out the women who wanted to leave their lives in vice behind them and take on proper, reputable work. If they were willing to try and leave their old lives behind then I would fund their training, re-education and so on."

"Fascinating; were you successful?"

"Not at first. We had a number of disappointments but Rose and I were determined and slowly, very slowly we began to see our labours start to bear fruit."

"Did you work with other similar groups?"

"No, Peter. The fact of the matter is that there were no other groups doing what we were doing, or rather trying to do. There were other groups but they all had other overarching aims and objectives. Some would approach the problem from a religious point of view, others from the aspect of the temperance movements. However, Rose and I were simply interested in getting the women away from their lives steeped in vice and thereby giving the women better, safer and more fulfilling lives."

"Were you involved in any other philanthropic endeavours?"

"Indeed we were. The beauty of our involvement was that we could do whatever we pleased. Other well-meaning groups were restricted and concentrated their endeavours in one particular area but Rose and I were not fettered by such bonds and we would look into any particular problem where we thought we might be able to do some good. And the real beauty was that our funding was nigh on limitless. I can give you an example of something we did that you would most certainly have heard about. Are you interested?"

Randan was quite enjoying himself. "Of course I am."

"Well, some time ago, not long after our marriage, I was chatting to a mother who lived in a village not far from Theobalds Park. She was an ordinary working-class woman married to a local builder. He was a skilled artisan who neither smoked nor drank to excess and they should have been able to live quite comfortably. However, her children were poorly-dressed and hungry. I offered her financial assistance but she was a proud woman and declined my offer. It seemed that the real problem was simply that her husband was unable to find sufficient work in the local area which would give them a decent lifestyle. When I made enquiries of the local trade organisations, they told me that nearly all the local building work had dried up through a lack of investment. A lack of investment meant no building projects and that in turn meant no work for the local artisans. No work meant no income and for many good people it seemed the only option would be the workhouse."

"How were you able to help?"

Now it was Valerie's turn to smile. "The area needed a large-scale building project, so I decided to provide one."

"Which was?"

"I decided to purchase Christopher Wren's Temple Bar from the City of London Corporation, dismantle it stone by stone and reassemble it once again at Theobalds Park where I thought it would make a marvellous entrance gate to the estate."

"That was you?"

"It most certainly was. I arranged to meet the owner of one of our local building firms in Fleet Street and I asked him what sort of work would be needed to restore the fortunes of our local artisans. He told me that it would require investment in some sort of large-scale building or engineering project. So I suggested that such a project might possibly be like moving a large structure from one location to another? He nodded in agreement. So I pointed at Temple Bar and enquired if that could be moved from where it then stood, at the junction of the Strand with Fleet Street to Theobalds Park, perhaps? He just looked at me as if I were mad."

"I can understand his shock. How did you arrange it."

"Once again, it was surprisingly easy. I had heard from Henry, who has his fingers in a great many pies, that the City Corporation were concerned that the old gate which had formed the boundary between the City of London and Westminster since its construction in the seventeenth century was now too narrow and was causing a huge obstruction to the free flow of goods and traffic along Fleet Street and the Strand. They had decided that Wren's Temple Bar would simply have to go. The problem seemed to be that they had no idea what to do with it. They knew that simply destroying a historic building would cause a huge public outcry and they had no idea of how to remove the obstruction without upsetting everyone. So I suggested to the Lord Mayor over dinner one night that Henry and I would solve this problem for the Corporation by purchasing the old gate (for a sensible price, of course). We would have it dismantled stone by stone and re-erect it in Hertfordshire – and so it was! The project was massive. It involved engineers, architects, surveyors and of course a huge work force which completely revived the fortunes of our local artisans."

"Which was, of course, your original intention."

"Correct! Plus it had one huge added advantage. It cemented my reputation in polite society that I was a completely eccentric lunatic who was intent on ruining Henry and possibly even bringing the whole Empire to its knees."

"I am in awe, Valerie, though I must say, I was very sorry to see that particular piece of history disappear from London."

"You just never know Peter. And I said to the Lord Mayor, Sir William McArthur when we signed the agreement, 'I would not be one bit surprised if Temple Bar one day makes a grand return to The City, but perhaps in a rather more convenient location!'" Valerie drew a deep breath "Well Peter, now you know who I am and how I came to be where I am."

"Yes, and it is indeed a fascinating story that you have to tell, but now tell me why you are here at New Scotland Yard and seeking the assistance of the Metropolitan Police. Is it to do with your philanthropic works?"

"Yes, it is. I told you earlier that Rose and I work with women involved in vice but who seek to turn their lives around. I told you that after a difficult start our work began to enjoy a fair degree of success. Word quickly spread amongst the women that Rose and I were fair and genuine women who wished only to assist them but who wouldn't preach or moralise to them. Rose and I agreed from the outset that we should be completely honest with the women because frankly, neither of us is exactly in a position to moralise to anyone; and to be honest, Peter, I think that is why we have succeeded where many others have failed. Rose and I can empathise with these women and slowly they have come to trust us not as 'do-gooding liberals' but as friends who are willing to assist those who have a genuine desire to improve their lives by moving away from the world of vice."

"I understand. You said earlier that you had some information? What is it that you have gone to all this trouble to tell me?"

Valerie drew another deep breath. "I think I may have evidence and information that relates to yet another serial murderer operating in London – Lambeth to be precise. Does that sound foolish coming from me?"

"Of course not. Tell me what you have found out."

"Rose and I have concentrated our efforts so far on working with women in the area of Lambeth and in the course of our work we have become close to a number of working women who we believe are genuine about changing their lives for the better. This is never achieved overnight; it all takes time. Sometimes a long time. We meet these women individually every week or so in a local coffee house where they feel comfortable, and we chat about their lives and families. Some of their stories touch even my stony heart, Peter. On October the 14th I had arranged a meeting with a young woman named Ellen Donworth, whom all the other women knew as 'Nellie'. She was a pretty young girl and only about 19 years old. In every respect she was fit, healthy and I would say that she was generally robust in every way. However, when I met her she looked terrible, she was as white as a sheet and she had been sweating profusely. She told me that she was fine and that she probably had a bad dose of influenza or something similar. As we chatted, I could see that she was suffering stomach pains and she complained of feeling sick. I asked her if she might be with child, but she said not."

"Did she tell you anything else"?

"Yes, after a few minutes her cramps eased and she relaxed a little. We don't tell all of the women we work with about our own personal histories but in order to gain their trust Rose and I have to let them know that we have at least a little personal knowledge of what their lives are like. Nellie was a bright and bubbly girl and she didn't mind telling us about her work. She would say that her dream was to meet a decent man who would take her away from her lifestyle and I am in absolutely no position to tell anyone that such a thing is impossible. Nellie told me that only the previous night she had met a man who she described as a 'really decent gent'. She told me that she had agreed to meet him after he had sent her a couple of letters. She said he was tall and quite good looking although she mentioned that he did appear to be a bit cross-eyed, but he was really smartly dressed and that he spoke in a very refined manner but with what she thought was an American accent. She said he claimed to be a doctor and he clearly made an impression on her. It seems they went to her room and everything had been quite normal."

Peter interrupted, "How do you mean 'Normal'?"

"I mean he did not request anything unusual, rough or exotic."

"Did she mention anything else about him?"

"Just one thing, but I shouldn't think it has a bearing. She mentioned that although he spoke in what she thought was an educated manner, when he laughed, it was in a very high pitched voice, almost like a screech, but that was all."

"I see, carry on."

"When he left, he said something to Nellie that was quite unusual, in fact she thought it a rather kind thought for a man in the medical profession. He told her that she looked rather pale and out of sorts and that could make her vulnerable to catching a chill in the damp autumn air. He took from his bag a bottle of porter and a tablet. He told her the drink would thicken her blood and that if she crushed the tablet and dissolved it in the drink it would 'pep her up'. Then he left. It seems she did as he advised and during the night she began to feel ill but she put it down to having caught something. Anyway, Nellie did not look at all well and I told her go and try to get some rest."

"What then?"

"I heard nothing further from her. The following week I had a meeting with another woman who knew Nellie quite well and she told me that poor Nellie had died on October 16th. It seems that her illness had just got worse after she left the coffee shop and it seems she passed away alone in her room. I felt terrible and that I should have called her a doctor, but it really did not seem too bad at the time."

"Was there a post-mortem examination of her body?"

"I suppose so, but nobody seems to think there was anything particularly unusual in her death."

"But you do?"

"Quite frankly, yes, I do. She was a young and healthy girl and not prone to sickness. I find it difficult to believe that she simply died of natural causes in just a few days."

"You said that you thought there may be a 'serial killer' loose in London. Are you aware of other unusual deaths?"

"Yes, at least one other. Nellie died on Friday, October. 16th and I heard about it on the following Thursday, October 22nd. On the next day, Friday, October 23rd, I was informed that another woman in our group had also died. Her name was Matilda Clover. She was older than Nellie and we all knew that she had a considerable drink problem. We had tried to offer her assistance but there was no denying she was an alcoholic and we were told that the official cause of her death was due to her alcoholism."

"But you doubt that?"

"Yes, I do. Matilda died in considerable pain on Wednesday, October 21st, but before she died she had spoken to another woman and she told her that she had met a man the previous night in a pub and that he had bought her several drinks before she took him to her room. She didn't think anything strange about it until she awoke in the middle of the night in dreadful pain. Her friend said that Matilda thought the man could have 'spiked' her drinks in the pub."

Again Randan interrupted her narrative. "That may be true. But it's only supposition at this time."

"I realise that, Peter, but I haven't finished yet. I asked her friend if Matilda had said anything else about this man and she had described him as a tall, handsome, well dressed and educated man with an American accent. Peter, I think we are talking about the same man in both cases and I believe he may have poisoned both Nellie and Matilda."

"That is a very large assumption, Valerie, and the evidence is very far from compelling. At the very best it is circumstantial.

It was Valerie's turn to interrupt him. "I realise that too, Peter, and that is exactly the reason why I am here talking to you. I want to officially put it on record that I believe two of my friends have been murdered and I want you to investigate both deaths and, if I'm correct, bring their murderer to justice."

When Valerie had finished speaking, she looked expectantly across the desk at Randan and he returned her gaze. "Well Peter, what do you think? Do you think I might be correct? Do you agree that we may have a killer stalking the streets of Lambeth?"

Peter remained silent and deep in thought for several seconds until Valerie almost shouted at him "*Well?*"

After his deliberation Randan answered her. "Valerie, I believe from what you have just told me that the deaths of Ellen Donworth and Matilda Clover need to be properly investigated by police. It needs to be established whether their deaths are, as you believe, 'suspicious' or whether their deaths can be explained in some other way. I do agree with you that the apparent involvement of the tall man with a possibly transatlantic accent should also be investigated. It could be that he has questions to answer. On the other hand, his involvement could be innocent and merely coincidental."

Valerie looked at him intently. "You think?"

Peter looked back at her with equal intensity "That is what a full investigation will reveal, and I must say, from a professional point of view, I will be most interested to hear the final conclusions of the investigating officer."

Valerie suddenly stood up with a look of absolute fury etched into her face and shouted across the desk "*What the hell did you just say?*"

Randan gazed across his desk with a look of total bemusement on his face at the enraged woman who had so suddenly replaced the calm figure who just a few seconds before had been narrating her story.

"Inspector Randan! Do you honestly imagine that I have come here today to bare my soul and share with you the most intimate details about my life, which by the way, I have never told to anyone else, not even those closest and dearest to me, in order for you to gossip and tittle tattle with your detective friends about me? Is that what you really think? If so, then I am afraid you are most gravely mistaken!"

Valerie now calmed and composed herself almost as rapidly as she had erupted and once more took her seat. "Dear lord, what a fool I have been! How could I have been so stupid as to imagine that I would come here and persuade you to help someone whom you met briefly so many years ago? *Stupid! Stupid! Stupid!*"

Now Valerie turned her face away from the dumbstruck police officer and almost whispered, "I apologise, Inspector, for having wasted your valuable time, I won't delay you any longer," and with that she rose to her feet and Randan could see the tears flooding down her cheeks.

Randan also rose smartly from his seat. "Please wait, your ladyship ... Valerie ... allow me to explain. Can I get you another cup of tea?"

Valerie spoke calmly but through gritted teeth "No, Peter, I do *not* want another cup of bloody tea. But, yes, please, go ahead and explain."

"You have provided a detailed account of what you know and I completely agree with you, these deaths demand further investigation. You have sought me out in the belief that because I am an inspector in the detective branch I can deal competently with this investigation. The truth is that perhaps once I could have done so, but those days are now, I fear, behind me. I have been stuck behind this desk for too long and I am out of touch with all of the modern aspects of detective work. The truth is that if I took this case I would probably let you down and be a huge disappointment to you. There are however many excellent senior detectives in London and any of them will do a better job than me and *that* is the truth. What I am willing to do is to arrange for you to pass on your information to a senior detective in Lambeth

Division for them to deal with your case. But please believe me, I would never gossip to anybody else about what you have told me about your past life. Those secrets are utterly safe with me, that I can promise you."

Valerie had watched Peter intently as he spoke and had now completely recovered her composure. "Thank you, Peter. I am certainly pleased that you don't think I have wasted your time; that means a lot to me. I don't believe, however, that you are no longer sufficiently competent enough to deal with these murders. But I suppose I should have realised that I can't just walk into New Scotland Yard and demand that you drop everything in order to assist me. Perhaps I was too much engaged in the past. All those years ago a young police constable put his own life at risk to help a young woman who thought that she was about to draw her last breath. A few days later that same officer returned wanting to persuade that young woman to give evidence and put that brute before a criminal court. Yet that young woman allowed herself to be persuaded to drop the matter and accept that violent assault is all part of a whore's job, an 'occupational hazard' if you will. I wish you could understand how much I now bitterly regret that decision."

"You weren't to know, Valerie. You did what you thought was right."

"No, Peter, I took the easy way out and perhaps I am still trying to make amends for that mistake all these years later by trying to obtain justice for Nellie and Matilda now. Anyway, thank you for your help and advice. I will, of course, accept your offer to hand this matter over to one of the local detectives at Lambeth, though I will never put the same trust in them as I have invested in you over all these years."

"They really are very good and entirely professional, Valerie, I can assure you of that."

"Yes, I am sure they are Peter. I'm equally sure that Chief Inspector Abberline was also very good and highly professional and yet he was completely ineffective in solving the Whitechapel Murders just a couple of years ago, wasn't he?"

"That was an incredibly difficult and complex case, Valerie."

"Indeed it was, Peter, as I'm sure were the Thames Torso Murders that took place in that same year. Doubtless that was also a difficult and complex case but do you know what both those cases have in common, Peter? Let me tell you; both cases involved the brutal killing and mutilation of women. Do you know what the common denominator was for every single one of those poor murder victims, Peter?"

"They were all prostitutes."

"Precisely, Peter every single one of those women was a prostitute and I expect that each of them had probably been told that violence against them was just another 'occupational hazard'. The good people of London have heard quite enough about dead prostitutes. They have now totally lost interest and the deaths of Nellie and Matilda won't warrant a single line in any of the national papers. The press had a field day with Jack the Ripper and were annoyed with the police for failing to put someone – anyone – in front of a judge and jury so that they could pore for eternity over the full salacious details. So; no more dead prostitutes in our newspapers. After all, who cares about them?"

"You and I care, Valerie."

"Do we, Peter? Do we really care enough? Tell me one thing. If things were different and if you were not stuck behind this desk, would you care enough to accept the investigation and go after this murderer?"

"If I was asked to, yes, I would."

Valerie stood up, smiled and offered her hand to the detective. "Thank you again, Peter. It seems that I made the right choice after all. I hope that we will meet again in the not too distant future. I really am delighted that your career has gone so well."

Peter also stood, smiled and shook her hand. "I am equally pleased that you have found happiness and security in your new life, Valerie. Truly, I am. I will make the required arrangements for you to meet with the Lambeth detectives."

"Thank you Peter. Don't worry, I can see myself out "

Randan saw her to the door and watched her walk towards the stairs. He would however have been surprised to see her not go down stairs to the exit. Instead she climbed up to the top floor and knocked on the door marked 'Commissioner of Police'. When the door swung open, Valerie entered to be met by Sir Edward Bradford's secretary who greeted her with a warm smile. "Good afternoon, Lady Meux, how lovely to see you again."

"Good afternoon, is Teddy in? I really would appreciate a very quick word with him."

"Yes of course Lady Meux. I will tell him you are here."

Robert Jeffries

Chapter Four

Valerie entered Commissioner Bradford's large office to be greeted by a beaming Sir Edward. "Oh, Teddy, thank you so much for agreeing to see me at such short notice. I really do so hate to distract you from your important work."

Sir Edward kissed her offered hand and replied, "Nonsense, Valerie. I only wish that all my distractions were as radiant as you. Now, to what do I owe the pleasure of this visit? This is twice in a matter of days; I really do feel honoured."

Valerie blushed and fluttered her eyelids at the old soldier "You are such a charmer, Teddy. Henry has warned me about you, you know!"

Sir Edward laughed "Oh, if only, Valerie! Maybe a few years ago you might have been in danger. But I fear I am now a little too old for amorous thoughts and your honour is quite safe with me. Now, what can I do for you? Is it related to your last enquiry?"

"Indeed it is, Teddy. Last time I asked you about an officer who assisted me some years ago and you discovered that he is indeed still a serving police officer."

"Yes, I think he is now an inspector in the detective branch. Didn't I tell you that his office is downstairs? Have you seen him yet?"

"Yes Teddy; in fact I have only just left his office. As I

told you last time, the reason I wanted to contact him again was in the hope that he might be able to assist me with a matter that I think is of significant importance to the police but is also a matter of some delicacy. I know from my past dealings with Inspector Randan that he is a man who possesses both great empathy and discretion."

"You evidently think very highly of this chap to go to so much trouble, Valerie. Was he able to offer you the help you need?"

Valerie smiled "He was indeed able to help me Teddy. He really is the ideal officer for this task. However, he did point out a couple of problems, which is why I have come to bother you again."

"You know very well that if I can be of assistance to you, then I will. Does this matter have anything to do with your work with 'fallen women' by any chance?"

"I can't get anything past your gaze, can I, Teddy? Yes, it does, though we prefer to use the terms 'distressed or vulnerable women' in our work."

"Can you tell me anything more? Or are you bound by confidentiality?"

"Not really, Teddy, I just don't want to take up too much of your valuable time so I'll be brief. During the course of our work, my colleague and I have uncovered what we think may be a serious criminal matter and we want to bring this to the notice of the police to be fully investigated."

"I see. How serious a criminal offence are we talking about, Valerie?"

"I suspect that two of our 'distressed women' may have been murdered, Teddy."

Sir Edward furrowed his brow. "Offences don't get much more serious than murder, do they? What did your inspector friend have to say about that?"

"I knew he would be highly concerned and supportive and he would very much like to investigate the matter further. However, he also pointed out a couple of problems as regards police procedure."

"Such as?"

"He pointed out that he was an officer employed to work in the Criminal Records Office and that serious allegations of the kind I am making would normally be dealt with by detectives working on the local division, in this case, Lambeth."

"He is absolutely correct there. That would normally be the appropriate way of proceeding. Why are you so intent on having your friend Randan handle this investigation? I'm quite sure there are several local officers who would be more than capable of handling this inquiry."

Valerie frowned a little and took his hand into hers "Teddy, darling. May I be completely frank and blunt?"

"Of course you can, Valerie. Anything you say to me will be strictly between us."

"Thank you so much, Teddy; I truly value that. I absolutely don't doubt the ability of your local officers to solve the case relating to these two unfortunate ladies, but as I said before, this investigation requires complete and absolute discretion. Our work with these distressed ladies is based on trust and confidence. Rose and I have worked long and hard to gain the acceptance of these women and I'm afraid that they simply don't trust the police and that is a fact. I hesitate to say this to you, Teddy, but the Metropolitan Police Force has not exactly covered itself in glory when it comes to investigating the murder of prostitutes over the last few years, have they? The reason why I need Inspector Randan to handle this inquiry is because I know I can rely totally not only on his detective ability but also on his honesty, integrity and discretion."

Sir Edward looked serious for a few seconds. "Very well, Valerie. I can see that this matter comes outside the normal remit of criminal investigations and that because of the special circumstances surrounding these two possible victims, there is a need to do things rather differently. Leave this matter with me for now and I will try and sort this out for you. Unless you hear differently from me beforehand, Inspector Randan will be able to assist you from tomorrow. Is that all right?"

Valerie threw her arms around his neck and hugged him tightly "Oh, Teddy, you are an absolute darling, and I *knew* I could trust you to assist me with this. I promise that you really are doing absolutely the best thing for all concerned with this decision of yours."

Sir Edward blustered a little. "Yes, I'm sure this will all turn out well. Leave it to me."

Valerie turned and left the office. She descended the stairs and left the building before hailing a hansom cab in Whitehall and returning to her apartment in Mayfair.

When Valerie had departed from his office, Randan stepped out of his own small office and walked over to Joan's desk. "How much of my conversation with Lady Meux did you overhear, Joan?"

"Hardly any, sir, except when she raised her voice towards the end – I imagine that most of New Scotland Yard would have heard that – but hardly anything else. I certainly didn't hear anything about her early life in London and how she came to work at the Casino de Venice. Or about how you rescued her from an attacker. Nothing like that. Or about those women she believes were murdered, sir. I was just getting on with my work, sir, as usual."

"That's good, Joan because if I did think that you may possibly have overheard any of those other conversations then I would have to remind you that you must never whisper a word to anyone about what you heard. But, since you didn't hear anything untoward, there will be no need for me to mention it again. Will there?"

"Absolutely not, sir."

Randan returned to his usual paperwork but as he worked through the files he couldn't help thinking about his recent unexpected visitor. Then his train of thought was broken by Joan handing him a message. "This just arrived for you, Mr Randan."

"Thank you, Joan" He opened the envelope and read the note inside and Joan immediately noticed an apprehensive look appear on his face.

"Bad news, sir?"

"I have no idea, Joan, but I imagine I will soon find out. This is certainly a day for surprises. I have just been summoned to the Commissioner's office."

"Sir Edward Bradford?"

"That's the one."

"What are you going to do?"

"Go up and find out what he wants, I suppose."

Five minutes later Peter Randan was standing outside the Commissioner's office feeling a bit like a naughty boy about to enter the headmaster's study to be reprimanded for some recently discovered misdeed. He straightened his tie and knocked on the door. "Inspector Randan to see Sir Edward."

"Go in, Inspector, he is expecting you."

Peter knocked on the closed door and entered Sir Edward Bradford's private office. "Slightly bigger than mine," he thought silently to himself before announcing himself to his senior officer. "Inspector Randan from CRO, sir; you sent for me?"

Sir Edward raised his eyes from the document in front of him and inspected his subordinate from over his spectacles. "Yes, Randan, thank you for coming so promptly. I understand that you are familiar with Lady Valerie Meux?"

"That is correct, sir. In fact she visited my office only this morning."

"Yes, I know. She's a fine woman, Randan, a damn fine woman and she seems to think very highly of you."

"That is most gratifying to know, sir. But the truth is our paths have only ever crossed once before this morning and that was many years ago."

"That is neither here nor there, Randan. The fact remains that she thinks highly enough of you to ask for your assistance in investigating what she believes may be a case of murder. Possibly even a double murder. She told you of her concerns?"

"She did indeed, sir, but I had to tell her that I was not in a position to take on an investigation that should normally be undertaken by the local detectives on Lambeth Division."

"Quite correct Randan. However, Valerie ... I mean Lady Meux ... has informed me that involving local officers in this investigation would almost certainly compromise and damage the valuable social work she performs with prostitutes ... I mean distressed women ... in the area. She believes that you would be more empathetic in your approach but would still be able to secure justice for the two dead women. She also tells me that you are keen to be involved. Is that the case?"

"I am prepared to do whatever I am instructed to do, Sir Edward, but taking on this investigation would inevitably mean that I wouldn't be able to spend as much time on my everyday work as I usually do."

"I understand Randan. Take the case and first of all let's find out if this really is a murder investigation. I suspect that Lambeth won't be overly impressed but I will explain the reasons to the superintendent there myself. Keep me personally updated on your findings. I think Lady Meux will be in contact with you again tomorrow. Is there anything else?"

"Not really, sir. I will clear my desk as best I can today and wait to speak to Lady Meux again tomorrow."

"Excellent. One other thing Randan. As I said earlier, Lady Meux is a very fine lady, the epitome of an English rose. Slightly eccentric, perhaps, but there is nothing wrong with that. How long have you been employed in CRO?"

"Over five years, sir."

"That's a long time for a detective. Have you chosen to stay there?"

"Not really, sir. It's just that I haven't had a chance to get out."

"Then you might want to look upon this as a chance to impress and I can assure you that if Lady Meux is impressed with your efforts, then I will be too. Do I make myself clear?"

"Crystal clear, sir."

Sir Edward considered Randan closely for a second. "Have you ever dealt with a killer who preys on women before, Randan?"

"No, sir; serious assaults but never a killer."

"You will need to tread carefully. The force was heavily criticised for its handling of the Whitechapel Murders and if this turns out be what Lady Meux fears then we can once again expect close scrutiny from the press. Especially if we fail to make an arrest and obtain a conviction. If you need assistance, don't hesitate to ask for it and I mean that. If this turns into a high profile investigation, you won't be criticised by me if you request help with your inquiries. I'd certainly prefer to offer you more manpower rather than give the press another field day at our expense."

"Let's get the investigation started, sir. Then I can assess what we might be facing."

"Excellent. Carry on, Randan."

"Thank you, sir."

Randan returned to his office and told Joan of his conversation with Sir Edward.

"Oh, this is just what you wanted, sir. A chance to prove yourself."

"Or a chance to fall flat on my face, Joan."

"No, sir. You are a good man and a talented detective. It's your chance to shine. Tomorrow is Saturday and it will be an excellent day to make a start on your inquiries, or at least to form a plan for your investigation.

"You are right, Joan. I'm going to go home and get my thoughts together tonight and formulate a plan tomorrow ready to start the investigation proper first thing on Monday morning."

"That's the spirit. You'll have this solved in no time."

"Let's hope so, Joan."

Saturday, October 24th 1891 at eight am saw Inspector Peter Randan of the New Scotland Yard Detective Branch bounding up the stairs to his office. He threw open the door into the general office and as expected saw Joan sitting at her desk. What he was not expecting was to see Lady Valerie Meux sitting next to her, tucking into a cup of tea and a buttered scone.

"Oh, good morning Peter, Joan said that you would be in at eight on the dot. I always think it is so awfully important for a man to be punctual."

Randan looked at the smartly dressed wife of a rich aristocrat. Yesterday she had been beautifully dressed, as if she was looking to make an impression. Today she was dressed less elegantly but looking as if she was about to go to a smart meeting of some description.

"Lady Meux ... Valerie. Forgive my look of surprise but I wasn't expecting to see you here this morning."

"Whyever not, Peter? If you and I are going to be working together to solve these murders, then the sooner we make a start, the better. I am here at your disposal to help in any way I can."

Randan stood looking at her with a bemused look on his face. "I beg your pardon. What did you just say?"

"Are you hard of hearing, Peter? I really had no idea. Doesn't that make being a detective somewhat awkward?"

"There is nothing wrong with my hearing, thank you. I was merely questioning your last statement."

"What? About me assisting with your investigation?"

"Precisely that! Absolutely not! It's completely impossible. Out of the question!"

"Oh dear. How tiresome. I was only just saying to Joan how I thought that you might be of that very mistaken opinion. Didn't I just say that to you, Joan?"

Joan looked up from her desk with more than the hint of a smile on her face. "Indeed you did, my lady."

"Joan did try and warn me that you may not be fully in agreement with this idea."

Randan sensed conspiracy in the air but decided to remain firm. "Joan was completely correct in her assertion. You have gone to a lot of trouble to secure my help in this matter, Valerie, but there your part in this investigation must begin and end. I work alone. We as yet have no idea where this investigation may lead and if we are indeed dealing with a murderer then I cannot possibly involve you in something that might put you in danger. What on earth would your husband say if he knew you were involved in a murder investigation?"

Valerie Meux had come prepared and ready for a fight but she was completely calm as she replied. "I know exactly what my beloved Henry would say, Peter – and I do know him a little better than you do, remember? He would tell me to follow my instincts and to make sure that this criminal is brought to justice!"

"I doubt he would say that if you were put in a position of danger!"

"Then don't put me in any danger, Peter! After all, what's the point of obtaining the assistance of a top New Scotland Yard detective if he can't protect one?" Valerie then smiled disarmingly at the detective. "Peter, there is one hugely important thing that you are overlooking."

"And what exactly is that, may I ask?"

"Peter, the question is not whether you can solve this investigation with my assistance. The real question is whether you can possibly solve this investigation *without* my assistance? The simple fact of the matter is that in order to successfully complete your inquiries you will have to enter the world of prostitution. You will have to speak to these women and - guess what? Most of them do not trust the police! The only way you will gain their assistance is with the help and assistance of Rose and me. We are your only gateway into their world and without us your inquiries are doomed to failure before you even start! Now, do you wish to stand here and argue with me further? Or shall we go upstairs and ask Teddy what he thinks? Because I think you know that he will agree with me."

Randan looked crestfallen. "This is most unusual," he protested.

"Oh, don't look so sorry for yourself, Peter. I think you will find that I have some very good ideas to take us forward. Joan and I were just discussing them, weren't we, Joan?"

"Erm, yes we were," she smirked."

Randan's sense of a female conspiracy against him grew

ever stronger.

The detective looked nervous and asked quizzically. "May I ask what these good ideas might be"?

"Of course you can, Peter. The first idea concerns which location we should use as a base for the investigation."

Again, Randan looked confused "Surely here is the obvious place to use, where else other than New Scotland Yard?"

"Yes, where else indeed" retorted Valerie. "Personally, I think your office here is a perfectly terrible place to use as our headquarters."

Randan replied quietly, "May I ask why?"

"Yes, Peter. It's a terrible idea *because* this is your office! This is the place where you do all your usual everyday work and while you are in this office it will be hugely difficult for you to concentrate on the greater matter at hand, that is catching our murderer. Surely you can see that?"

"Valerie, I just can't simply forget about my job here. I have to continue my work here alongside working on this other investigation."

"Yes, I know that and it is somewhat annoying, *but* I really do think it is essential to separate your two roles and to that end I do have some suggestions. First of all, I have already had a word with dear Teddy, and he has agreed to lend you a sergeant and he will be able to carry on the bulk of your office work while you are otherwise employed. I suggest that you only really need to pop into the office here once or twice a week to check that everything is alright. After all, I would not want the important office work of New Scotland Yard to grind to a halt just because their most efficient and diligent detective is involved in something else. Besides, Peter, we must also look to the future here and it is only right and proper that you should have another officer trained up and ready to take over your work here when it becomes time for you to move somewhere else. Isn't that so, Joan?

Joan nodded sagely.

Once again Randan appeared to be confused "I'm sorry. Move on? Why would I be moving on?"

"Oh *do* concentrate, Peter! If I am correct in asserting that the two deaths are both connected murders, then solving the case and bringing the culprit to justice will be a huge feather in the investigating officer's cap. Or in your case in his brown derby! I think it highly likely that once you solve these murders …"

"Alleged murders, Valerie!"

"Have it your way, Peter, 'alleged murders'! Once you have solved them, I think I can confidently predict that you will be Chief Inspector Peter Randan. It has a certain ring to it, don't you think, Joan?"

"Oh, definitely, Lady Meux!"

Both women smiled sweetly at the detective.

"You still have not said where you think we should use as a base for our inquiry?"

"Have I not? Oh dear, how remiss of me. I suggest we use the Savoy Grill, it will be the perfect location."

"The Savoy Grill? Have you taken leave of your senses?"

Valerie pouted and looked hurt. "Why no, I don't believe so. Why do you say that?"

"Because this may be a murder inquiry. The Savoy Grill is a restaurant. You simply can't use a restaurant as a base for a murder enquiry. It's a ridiculous idea!"

"Peter, how many clients of the Savoy Grill do you know personally?"

"None."

"Precisely. You know absolutely nothing about the place. I on the other hand, know a large number of them and I also know that many of them use the Grill as a base for their businesses and social entertaining. It is pleasant, comfortable, and incredibly discreet. I don't think there is anything in the police rule book that says investigating detectives and their staff must not have any degree of comfort whilst involved in investigations, is there?"

"No, I suppose not. There is however a rule that says inspectors must not frequent restaurants that are well and truly out of their price range."

Valerie smiled warmly "Oh, Peter, don't be such a stick in the mud! I have no intention of reducing you to a state of penury. All refreshments will be on my account and they will all be properly recorded so there is no question of impropriety on your account. Also, It will all be cleared with Teddy, just to make sure that we are within the rules."

Randan only had to glance at Joan to know that she was all in favour of this plan of action.

Valerie stood up and said, "Now all that is left is for us to stroll along the Embankment to the Savoy and introduce you both to Joseph, the Maitre d'hotel at the Grill. Once that is done, we are free to proceed and you will both be able to use my booth whenever you need to."

"It's really as easy as that?" queried Randan.

"Absolutely!" replied Valerie with a smile.

An hour later, Valerie, Randan and Joan were seated in Valerie's private booth sipping tea. Valerie had introduced them both to Joseph who now treated them as old and valued friends. Joan simply could not stop grinning. "Now, will you concede that this was a good idea, Peter?"

"Let's just wait and see how everything turns out, shall we?"

Valerie put her hand to her mouth in an exaggerated action and said to Joan as an aside, "I think that is police slang for 'Yes', Joan."

Even Randan was forced to grin. "Since we are officially here on business, I suppose we should discuss some sort of plan."

"Absolutely; what do you have in mind?"

"I shall spend the rest of the day examining what paperwork exists for the two deaths in question and on Monday I shall pay a visit to the Southwark Coroner's office and find out what he can tell me about the deaths. Once I have done that, I should be able to decide whether either or both of the deaths should be viewed as 'Suspicious'. And as soon as I have done *that*, I will contact you immediately.

Valerie peered across the perfectly laundered tablecloth at the detective and placed one hand on his and her other over Joan's hand. "I want you both to understand exactly how much your taking on this investigation means to me." She turned to Joan. "Joan, I won't insult your intelligence. I know that you heard most, if not all, of my first conversation with Peter the other day, so you already know quite a lot about my history and how Peter and I first became acquainted. I know you heard the conversation because if I had been in your position I would have made damn sure that I knew exactly what was going on. What is more, it is absolutely right and proper that you know. I have nothing to hide and I am ashamed of and regret absolutely nothing that has happened in my life. However, now I am in a position to do something good and positive with my life and I *know* in my heart that Peter, with your help and assistance, Joan, is exactly the right man for the job."

Joan simply answered, "I am sure that Inspector Randan and myself will both do whatever we can to get to the bottom of this, your ladyship.

Valerie looked straight at Joan, "Joan, I am a very well dressed and frightfully well-spoken ex whore. Please, just call me Valerie.

Robert Jeffries

CHAPTER FIVE

At ten in the morning of Monday, October 26th, Inspector Randan entered Southwark Coroner's Office, presented his warrant card to the court attendant and asked to see Dr. Pullman, the Coroner for Southwark and Lambeth. A few minutes later he was admitted into a well-lit office where the coroner was seated on the other side of a large oak desk scribbling on a sheet of paper.

"Thank you for seeing me at such short notice, sir."

"Not at all Inspector, how may I be of assistance?"

"I am looking into the recent death of two women, sir. The first one is one Ellen Donworth who died, I believe on the 16th of this month."

Before he could continue with the second name, he noticed that the coroner had removed his spectacles and was now staring at him with a look of considerable surprise on his face.

"Is something wrong, sir?" queried Randan.

"Indeed not, Inspector. However, I feel I must commend the speed and efficiency of your organisation!"

Now it was Randan's turn to look surprised. "Why so?"

"Simply because it has only been some twenty minutes since I began to wonder if I should contact the police regarding the cases of Miss Donworth and Miss Clover and quite frankly I was wondering who I should be speaking to about them. Now you appear to have resolved my dilemma."

Randan raised his eyebrows and continued, "Why might you feel that you need to contact the police regarding these ladies, sir? Have you come across anything unusual regarding this matter? Something suspicious, perhaps?"

Dr. Pullman allowed a slight smile to form on his lips and replied "Unusual? Yes most certainly. Suspicious? I'm not really sure, Inspector, and that is why I wanted to seek police advice."

"What have you found unusual regarding the death of these women, sir?"

"To be frank Inspector, until this morning absolutely nothing. The autopsy examination of Ellen Donworth proved inconclusive and revealed nothing particularly unusual in the death of a young woman involved in Miss Donworth's profession. I'm assuming that you are aware that she was a prostitute?"

Randan nodded his assent. "So, what have you discovered today that has caused you to be concerned enough to want to contact the police?"

The coroner lifted a letter from his desk and handed it to the detective. "Tell me, Inspector, have you ever come across anything like this before?"

Randan reached across the desk and accepted a letter which had been typed onto a sheet of note paper. "I will read it out loud, Doctor and please interrupt if you wish to. 'My Dear Dr Pullman, please excuse this unsolicited communication but I feel it is my duty to contact you in this way to ensure justice for people whom I fear can no longer speak for themselves. I regret to say that I am presently unable to reveal to you my identity for reasons that will become clear later in this missive, but suffice it to say for now that like you, I am a qualified physician. I am given to understand that you are presently looking into the circumstances surrounding the death of two women, Ellen Donworth, known to her associates as 'Nellie' and Matilda Clover. I believe that these ladies passed away on October 16th and October 20th of this year. I am sure that autopsies have already been performed by your pathologist and I strongly suspect that he has found very little out of the ordinary. However, it has come to my attention that both of these unfortunate ladies were in fact victims of a cunning and ingenious murderer who took their lives by means of administering a toxic substance and I am sure that when your pathologist reviews his examination with a view to looking specifically for toxins, he will find the relevant evidence in their tissues. Furthermore, I am in position to reveal to you and the relevant authorities, the identity of this dastardly murderer. I mentioned earlier that I am not in a position to reveal my own identity to you in this letter. This is because, through no fault of my own, I find myself in a state of severe financial embarrassment and with that in mind it is with great regret that I find myself in need of asking for financial reward in exchange for my knowledge and expertise. I strongly believe that the information and evidence that I am able to provide will bring about the conviction of this terrible murderer and that the sum I request (£300,000) is but a small price to pay for ending this criminal's reign of terror. I use that term certain in the knowledge that if he is allowed to escape justice on this occasion, he will most assuredly strike again. Indeed, who can say if he has not already killed again? I am quite sure that there is no need for me to remind you of the degree of distrust and anger that will be felt by the public and the press if it comes to light that yet another murderer is at large and unchecked on the streets of London following the shocking failures of the police investigations during the Whitechapel Murders. It may even be imagined in some quarters that the Whitechapel Murderer is once again abroad on our streets and that thought might well provoke outbreaks of further violence. Once you have obtained the required permission from the authorities, we can then make arrangements for how the money and information will be exchanged. I must stress that failure to comply with my entirely reasonable request will mean that you will not hear from me again and if and when this murderer strikes again, the resulting loss of life/lives will be entirely the responsibility of whosoever has failed to work with me in this matter. I will contact you again shortly with further instructions Yours Sincerely, A. O'Brien (Detective)'"

The coroner reached back across the table for the letter but Randan was not letting go of it. "I think I will need to keep hold of this letter, sir."

"You think it's genuine then?"

"I think it is evidence in the case, sir."

"I see. What about his £300,000?"

"His demand amounts to blackmail, sir and I can't imagine anyone in authority wishing to pay such a large amount of money to an extortionist."

"But you read the letter, Inspector. If we fail to agree to his demands, then any further deaths will be our responsibility!"

"Wherever the responsibility lies, sir, it will not be with you. You have quite correctly brought the letter to the notice of 'the relevant authorities' exactly as he requested. I will deal with it from here."

Dr. Pullman looked concerned. "The autopsy on Donworth was inconclusive, Inspector, but the pathologist was far more certain that Clover's death was due to natural causes. She was a chronic alcoholic and the pathologist found high levels of alcohol in her body during his examination." The coroner leafed through a pile of files in a wire tray on his desk and pulled one out. "Ahh, here we are." He quickly read the entries. "She was also a prostitute but the pathologist discovered advanced cirrhosis of the liver and he states here that this was the main cause of her death after yet more heavy drinking."

"That may well indeed be the case, sir, but in the light of what this letter contains and also from other information that I am aware of, I will have to ask that your pathologist re-examines both women with a view to checking specifically whether poisons or other noxious substances may have been administered to either or both of them."

The look of concern on Dr. Pullman's face became even more evident. "Do you really believe that we are dealing with a murderer here, Inspector?"

"I really can't say for certain, sir and I am keeping an open mind for now. However, it is looking increasingly as if foul play may be involved and that is why it is so important that these re-examinations take place and if we are indeed dealing with a murderer, then I have no need to tell you, Doctor, time is of the essence!"

"I will ensure that the re-examinations are performed by tomorrow, Inspector."

"Thank you, sir; here is my card. Please contact me at the Yard as soon as your pathologist completes the second post-mortems."

Pullman looked at the offered card and there was a hint of surprise in his tone. "Inspector Randan of the Criminal Record Office?"

"Yes, sir. It's a long story."

Randan left the office of the Southwark Coroner, walked towards the Thames and turned left on the river footpath. The weather was fine and mild for October and he decided to walk to the Savoy where he had promised to meet Valerie and Joan.

As he walked towards Blackfriars Bridge, he considered what to do with the letter in his jacket pocket. He knew that if he went into the Savoy with the letter about his person, Valerie would want to look at it, and that niggled at his mind. Although he had agreed to work with Valerie he must also remember that he was a police officer and she was not. The letter may yet prove to be valuable evidence in this investigation and it should be treated as such.

Instead of turning right and crossing over Blackfriars Bridge, he climbed the stairs and crossed over Blackfriars Road, taking care to avoid the line of horse drawn carts and carriages making their way across the bridge towards the City. He then descended the stairs on the upriver side of the bridge and made his way along Bargehouse Alley. He continued along the footpath until Hungerford Bridge where he crossed the river via its pedestrian footpath. He then descended the stairs to the Victoria Embankment and continued towards Parliament before entering New Scotland Yard by its rear entrance.

It had taken him a little under twenty five minutes to reach New Scotland Yard, but that time had given him the chance to think. Instead of going directly to his office, he instead entered the property office and acquired a manilla property envelope from the stationery cupboard. With the envelope in his hand, he took the steps two at a time and swiftly arrived at his second-floor office. When he entered the office, he half expected to see Joan at her desk but he knew that she would now be with Valerie and probably enjoying a cup of tea in the Savoy Grill. In her place was a young sergeant in plain clothes who had been appointed by Sir Edward to cover their absence.

The sergeant stood up smartly as Randan appeared through the door. "All correct, sir, no reports. I wasn't expecting to see you today, sir. I assumed you would be fully involved with your investigation."

"Thank you, Sergeant, I have been involved with the investigation, but I have acquired some evidence and I really do need to book it in before doing anything else."

"Is there anything I can do to help, sir? It's fairly quiet here this morning."

"Yes, probably, Sergeant; just give me a couple of minutes, will you?"

The sergeant nodded his agreement and Randan opened his own office door and sat at his desk. He took out his pen and filled out the relevant information on the envelope. He then removed the letter from his inside jacket pocket, placed it into the manila envelope, closed the flap and then sealed it with a generous blob of red sealing wax. When he re-entered the other office, he handed the sealed envelope to the young sergeant and said, "Can I ask you to go down to the property office at some stage today and book this envelope into the overnight property cupboard. It really will be a great help."

"Of course, sir; do you mind if I ask a question, sir?" The question was asked almost nervously.

"It rather depends on what the question is, Sergeant."

"I was just wondering sir. It's just that I've heard some quite unusual things about your investigation, sir."

"Have you, Sergeant. What have you heard?"

"Well, sir. I've heard that you are working on an investigation under the direct authority of the Commissioner himself, sir."

"That is true, Sergeant. Anything else?"

"I've heard that you are working with a beautiful and very aristocratic lady, sir."

"Once again, your information is correct, Sergeant. Is that it?"

"One more thing, sir. They say you are using the Savoy Grill as a headquarters, sir, and that this lady is one of the richest people in the whole country, sir."

Randan was now smiling, "Once again Sergeant, your information is impeccable, and shall I tell you one other thing that you may not know?"

The young sergeant nodded in surprise that he would be confided in by his senior.

"Well, Sergeant," Randan looked both left and right and then almost whispered conspiratorially, "This lady I'm working with, Sergeant – she drives a carriage around London that is pulled by zebras!"

The sergeant's jaw dropped open in complete amazement and with that Randan left the office without a further word and was still laughing to himself as he left the building.

He was still smiling as he entered the Savoy Grill restaurant and was greeted by Joseph, the Maitre d'hotel who escorted him to Valerie's booth. "I think Lady Meux and her guest are keen to hear your news, Inspector. They have been most eagerly awaiting your arrival. I trust it has been a successful morning for you, sir."

"I think we have made progress thank you, Joseph."

Randan took his seat and Joseph left to arrange a pot of tea for the new arrival. "Tell me Valerie, am I being paranoid or does Joseph know exactly what we are investigating here?"

Valerie laughed "You are not the first to imagine that Joseph either has second sight or a direct line of communication with the Almighty! The truth is that neither is really the case but he is a highly intelligent man who is exceptionally good at his job. He works tirelessly and very little ever escapes his attention. Fortunately, he is also the absolute soul of discretion and any information or secrets that may come to his attention are completely and utterly safe. His booth has been described as keeping more secrets than a confession box. Now, tell us, Peter, what happened this morning and why has it taken so long?"

A waiter arrived with a pot of tea and Randan waited for the cup to be poured before beginning his story.

"I apologise for keeping you both waiting, but I decided to drop off some possible evidence at the office before coming here and that cost me time."

"Evidence?" said Valerie. "Perhaps you had better start at the beginning and tell us everything."

Randan related what had occurred in the coroner's office and repeated almost verbatim the contents of the letter from the person who simply referred to himself as A. O'Brien (Detective).

"Can I see the letter, Peter? Do you still have it on you"?

Randan shook his head. "No, the letter itself is the evidence that I needed to book in at the office."

"Couldn't you have brought it here first, Peter?"

"No, Valerie. The letter may or may not be important evidence and if it does become vitally relevant to the investigation, then I want to be able to show that we have handled it properly. I will have to ask you to trust me on matters of procedure. They may be annoying but while I am running this investigation then things will be done strictly according to the rules."

Valerie pouted at the detective "I suppose you're right, Peter. It's just that I have such vivid memories of a young police officer who achieved exceptional results but didn't necessarily achieve his objectives by sticking strictly to the rules."

Randan smiled back. "True. But that was a long time ago and back then we were not investigating possible murders."

Valerie arched her eyebrows. "So, you now believe that Nellie and Matilda's deaths were indeed murders?"

"I believe that remains a strong possibility. We should have a much better idea after the pathologist has completed his re-examination of the bodies."

"When will that be?"

"They should be completed by tomorrow. He will only be looking for the presence of toxins in the bodies."

Joan interrupted. "Shouldn't the pathologist have found the toxins during his initial examination, sir?"

"In a perfect world, Joan, yes he would have, but this is not a perfect world. Pathologists are overworked and always working against time. Therefore, if there is no reason to suggest that any given death is due to ingesting a noxious substance then he probably won't actually look for such evidence, particularly in the case of a woman like Matilda who was already suffering from a chronic and probably ultimately fatal illness."

"What Peter is trying to say, Joan" broke in Valerie, "is that when a pathologist is examining a dead prostitute, he may not be overly concerned with how she met her end. After all, as long as her corpse has not been violently abused, dismembered or disarticulated what does it really matter what actually caused her death? And who cares, anyway? Isn't that true, Peter?"

"That's not what I said, Valerie. But your point may have some validity."

Robert Jeffries

Chapter Six

Randan endured a restless night's sleep at his rented lodgings in Islington. By five thirty the next morning he was washed, dressed and heading along Upper Street towards the Angel Underground Station. He took the first southbound train and changed at Bank for another train to Westminster where he alighted. As usual, he checked his pocket watch against the huge dial of the clock on the tower of the Palace of Westminster and then proceeded on to New Scotland Yard.

At six thirty he fully expected to have the office to himself but as he opened the office door, he was amazed to see Joan already going about her work. "Good heavens Joan, I wasn't expecting to see you in at this time of the morning!"

Joan smiled at her senior officer and replied, "I couldn't sleep either, sir. I've just made a pot of tea; would you like a cup? I rather expected that you might be in early today."

"And what, may I ask, made you think that?"

"The look on your face when you were explaining to Lady Meux about that letter sent to the coroner. That and the fact that I know very well you will want to be here when the coroner tells you he has the results of the second post-mortems on our two victims."

"Sometimes I think that you should be running this office, Joan. Nothing escapes your scrutiny. You would make an excellent detective."

Again Joan smiled "Well, we both know that will never happen, sir. But who knows? One day women might be able to join the police and become detectives too! But not in my time, I'm afraid. Besides, I needed to come in and just check that everything is going smoothly here, and I can't do that from the Savoy Grill, lovely though it is."

Randan laughed. "I thought you would be putting in an application for our office to be relocated to the Savoy Grill, Joan."

"No, sir. It is nice to see how the other half live and they are all very polite to us, but it can't last, can it, sir? Once you have solved this case we will be back to normal again. Well, I will, anyway."

Randan noted a trace of sadness in her voice "What do you mean, Joan?"

"Nothing Mr. Randan. It's really none of my concern and I should not have said it."

"Come on Joan, what is worrying you?"

Joan sighed deeply "Very well, sir. You and Lady Valerie have a history, I know that. I also know that she is very taken with you and once you have solved this case she will keep her promise and persuade the Commissioner to promote you and you will be out of this office and on to ... well, who knows what? But I will still be here ... and .... I will miss you, sir!" Joan had to sniff back a little tear.

Randan was touched by her show of emotion and by her staunch loyalty to him. He reached over and took hold of her hand. "Dear Joan, there are an awful lot of ifs and buts in your theory. But let's get somethings absolutely clear. This case is a very long way from being solved. We can't even be certain that this is a murder enquiry just yet. Secondly, Lady Meux does not run the Metropolitan Police and though she undoubtedly does have a friendship and maybe some influence with the Commissioner that does not mean that he will be overriding existing protocols when it comes to promoting a lowly inspector. Even if he does solve a murder case. Finally, and most importantly, if I should be promoted and my career moves on, I will still need my faithful and highly trusted personal assistant by my side, if only to keep my feet planted firmly on the ground!"

Joan smiled and dabbed away the tear from her cheek. "You really are a kind man – " but before Joan could finish her sentence, the office door opened and Valerie Meux entered the room.

"Oh, I say, I am most dreadfully sorry. I really should have knocked! Am I interrupting something?"

Joan pulled her hand back as her cheeks reddened. "No, no," she stammered. "You haven't interrupted anything at all, Lady Meux."

"It's Valerie, remember?"

"Yes, of course, sorry, Lady ... I mean Valerie. Oh dear."

Randan was now smiling broadly "No, Valerie, you have not interrupted anything. Joan was telling me how much she will miss me when I am a famous detective and she remains stuck in the Criminal Records Office and I was assuring her that whatever the future may hold, she will not be getting rid of me anytime soon."

"Oh, I see," responded Valerie. "May I just point out to you both that *all* of our futures rather depend on us catching a murderer. Do we have any news yet?"

Randan shook his head and said, "Not yet. Cup of tea? And welcome to the humdrum world of everyday policing – waiting for something to happen."

The three of them sat around the office drinking several cups of tea.

"By the way, Valerie, what on earth are you doing here at seven in the morning?" he enquired.

"The same as both of you, I imagine. I had difficulty sleeping last night and decided to head for the Savoy Grill where I assumed I would find you two. When Joseph informed me that he had not seen either of you yet, I put two and two together. That's what you detectives do, isn't it, Peter? The answer I arrived at told me that I would probably find you here, drinking this barely passable tea rather than the wonderful brew that Joseph provides for us. Which brings me to ask why are you here? I thought we had agreed on using the Savoy Grill as our headquarters?".

"The Savoy Grill is a wonderful place, Valerie, but unfortunately Joan and I can't keep track of our more mundane work there. If you recall, we agreed that Joan and I would come in to check our normal work whenever the investigation allowed us the time. Today is such a time. There is nothing to do until I receive word from Dr. Pullman at Southwark and he will contact me here, in my office."

Valerie audibly 'harrumphed' as she shrugged her shoulders. "Oh, I suppose so," she allowed.

Joan had now recovered from her embarrassment "Lady … I mean, Valerie, may I ask you a question? If you don't mind, that is."

Valerie looked amused and replied, "Yes of course you may, Joan, what do you want to know?"

Joan thought for a second, wanting to phrase her question very carefully in her mind. "Well, you have led such a wonderfully adventurous life and you have done so many things that most people could never imagine doing, but do you ever get disappointed and frustrated with other people?"

Valerie smiled broadly. "Oh, my dear Joan! Of course I do! Just because I am now a woman of considerable means does not make me immune to everyday feelings and emotions. I regularly get frustrated by rich people who assume superiority *just* because they have money, but, to balance that out, I also get frustrated by poor people who assume they are worthless *just* because they don't have much money. But most of all, I get frustrated by sheer stupidity, arrogance and ignorance which I see evidence of all around us every day regardless of how wealthy people may or may not be. So, yes, I am very often disappointed."

"Could you give me an example?"

"An example? Oh, goodness, now you are putting me on the spot!" Valerie thought for a second. "Do you remember a case that made the newspapers about a dozen years back? It concerned an American artist named James McNeil Whistler. He became embroiled in a dispute with an art critic named

John Ruskin who had made some rather spiteful remarks about one of Whistler's paintings."

Joan looked blank. "I'm afraid art is not something that I know much about."

Randan gave a more positive response. "I do seem to recall something about that. I believe Whistler sued Ruskin for his comments and I also believe he actually won his case but the judge awarded such a small sum in damages that it left Whistler bankrupt and almost penniless after paying his legal fees. Am I right?"

"Absolutely correct, Peter. The judge awarded Whistler a farthing in damages and it left him stony broke. Now, the thing is that everybody connected with Whistler advised him to simply ignore the stupid comments. Everyone knew how talented he was as an artist, but Whistler knew better. He believed that this case would be the making of him as a famous artist and he insisted on following it through to the bitter end and it ruined him, not just financially but physically and mentally as well."

Randan looked quizzically at Valerie. "I remember the case, Valerie, but where do you come into the story?"

"I will tell you, Peter. I was a great admirer of Whistler's work and when I heard that he was left without funds or friends, I asked Henry if we might commission him to do some work for us. Henry agreed and I approached Mr. Whistler with that very idea. Now you must remember that after the court case Whistler had no work and very little prospect of getting any. I proposed that he should paint three different portraits of me. He could hardly believe his luck and accepted the commission which, needless to say, made him solvent once again. I sat for the first two portraits in his studio and I have to say that he did a wonderful job. His portraits of me were stunning and Henry was highly delighted with his work. When you sit as a model for an artist, Joan, the process does take rather a long time and during the long hours alone together we talked about all manner of things and I may have hinted to Mr. Whistler, or Jimmy as I used to call him, perhaps a little more than I should have about my life before

I married Henry. It is certainly not a mistake that I have made again! Anyway, the first two portraits were completed, and everything was wonderful. Jimmy sent me a note saying that he was ready to commence work on the third and final portrait whenever I was ready. We set a date and time and I went to his studio in Chelsea. At first everything was fine, he started his preparatory work and we slipped into the same casual friendliness that had been present during the first sittings. However, as work continued, I noticed a change in Jimmy's attitude and demeanour towards me. His friendly politeness changed to a sort of haughty aloofness. I decided to ignore it and put it down to his 'artistic temperament'. Then one afternoon he went too far and made lewd comments about my past and I'm afraid I lost my temper and flew into a rage. My carefully cultured accent was lost in my fury and suddenly I felt as if I was back in the Casino de Venice. I think I shouted at him 'You keep a civil tongue in your head, Jimmy Whistler, or I'll send someone round here to finish your paintings for you once and for all!' Or something very similar. It was an outright threat of violence and I meant every single word of it! And Jimmy knew it too. The look on his face was a picture of hurt pride! He raged and he postured at me then he insulted me again as I put on my coat, walked out and slammed the door behind me. I could hear Jimmy still shouting as I walked past his studio window and when I looked through the window, I could see him destroying the painting. Now that was extremely disappointing, Joan; does that answer your question?"

Joan gazed at Valerie with her mouth wide open "That was terrible, did you get your money back?"

"No, Joan, I never did. But Jimmy Whistler gave me something that was worth far more to me than the few pounds that he kept in his paint box; my self-respect! Therefore I will always remain grateful to him for teaching me a valuable lesson, although I suspect Jimmy will never understand that fact"

Just as Valerie completed her story, the office door opened and a messenger entered the room. "Inspector

Randan"?

Randan acknowledged.

"The Backhall Inspector has told me to give you this card, sir".

Randan glanced at the card from Dr Pullman, Southwark Coroner. On the reverse of the card it said simply, "Both results have been returned. Suggest you attend as soon as possible."

As he put on his jacket and reached for his hat he said to Joan and Valerie, "I will see you both at the investigation headquarters as soon as I can."

As Randan moved purposefully towards the office door Valerie rose to her feet. Joan stretched out her arm and gently took Valerie's arm "Valerie, I have been meaning to say. That really is a lovely outfit you are wearing today, it must have cost a lot of money."

Valerie looked puzzled "Thank you, Joan, It is a favourite of mine. But I really must catch up with Peter."

Joan kept a gentle hold of her elbow. "You've never visited a mortuary before, have you?"

"No, Joan, but what's that got to do with it?"

"You will never be able to wear that lovely jacket and skirt again, you know? You will never get the stench of the mortuary out of those fibres."

Valerie stopped in her tracks. "Really?"

Joan nodded wisely. "Yes, really".

"Well, perhaps we should let Peter get on with his work. I really would not want to get in his way and hinder the investigation."

Joan smiled. "I think that is a very sensible decision. Shall we have another cup of tea here or shall we wait until we get to the Savoy Grill?"

"Let's go and see what Joseph has on the menu today, shall we? It must be well past breakfast time."

By the time the two women reached the Victoria Embankment, Randan was already out of sight.

Randan had left New Scotland Yard by a gate that took him

directly onto the Victoria Embankment. One glance at the constant stream of slow-moving traffic was enough to inform him that his quickest way of getting to Southwark Coroner's Office would be on foot.

He dodged the traffic as he crossed the road to the riverside pavement. He barely noticed the huge granite obelisk known as Cleopatra's Needle as he walked quickly towards Blackfriars Bridge.

Twenty-five minutes later, he arrived at the coroner's office. The same man as the previous day acknowledged his warrant card. "Just knock and go in, sir, He's expecting you."

Randan did exactly that. "Thank you for coming so quickly, Inspector," said Dr Pullman.

"Not at all, sir, thank you for expediting the re-examinations so swiftly."

"In such circumstances as these, Inspector, I really had no option. As you said yesterday, time was of the essence."

"The results, sir; what did the pathologist find this time?"

Dr. Pullman's expression was serious. "I'm afraid you were quite correct, Inspector. Both women's bodies reveal traces of strychnine poisoning and in both cases the dose administered was the cause of death. You are definitely looking for a murderer."

Randan looked equally serious. "I feared as much, sir."

"Do you want to see the bodies, Inspector?"

"Yes, sir. That might be useful."

The two men left the coroner's office and made their way to the mortuary where the attendant was awaiting their arrival. Randan observed two marble tables in the room, each with white sheets covering them. The attendant withdrew both sheets to reveal the naked bodies of the two murdered women.

Pullman gestured towards them. "Donworth is on the left and Clover on the right. You can see that Donworth is the younger of the two. We believe that she was only 19 years old when she was murdered. You can see that although Clover is only eight years or so older than Donworth, she looks considerably older. Mostly through the effects of alcohol and abuse suffered during her years on the streets."

"They both represent a damning indictment of our times, Doctor. Were photographs taken during the examination? They may help with tracing her next of kin."

"Yes, of course." Pullman nodded to the attendant who pulled the sheets back over the two women once again as Randan and Pullman left the mortuary and returned to Dr. Pullman's office.

"Inspector, I don't mean to interfere with your investigation but now we know that the letter writer was correct in his claim that Donworth and Clover were both murdered, will that alter your investigation?"

"In what way, sir?"

"I mean, might you now be forced to take his claims more seriously and perhaps even agree to pay him the money he is demanding. Can you imagine the press and public response if you fail to pay him the money he is demanding and the murderer strikes again? This puts the police in a very difficult place!"

"Yes, sir, it does and fortunately it will not be my decision as to whether the authorities agree to pay the blackmailer who calls himself O'Brien or not. However, if the people making the decision ask for my advice, then I will have to advise them *not* to pay the money."

"I understand your feelings as a police officer, Inspector. However, sometimes, surely, we need to see the bigger picture and do what is in the public good. No matter how obnoxious that might seem at the time."

Randan paused for a couple of moments before replying. "Let us hypothesise for a moment, Doctor. Let us assume for the purpose of this exercise that everything O'Brien says in his letter is true. Let us also assume that he really has somehow stumbled upon information that led him to write the letter that you received. Let us also assume that he knows not only who murdered Ellen Donworth and possibly Matilda Clover but also how the murderer killed these two unfortunate women. Now finally let us also assume that the authorities decide to authorise the payment of the £300,000 in order to obtain that information. We must now ask ourselves if O'Brien or whatever his name really is, actually *does* provide us with all that information and enable the police to go and arrest the man he alleges is responsible for these murders and put him before a court. What will be the first question asked by his defence barrister?"

The doctor stared blankly. "I really have no idea, Inspector."

"The first question asked by any competent barrister will be 'How did the police gain their evidence?' The prosecution would then have to reveal that they had paid an extortionist for the information. And even the most junior barrister in the country could hardly fail to drive a coach and horses through all of the evidence obtained by paying O'Brien his £300,000. In other words, sir, his evidence would in all probability be inadmissible in a court of law."

"But surely, if he *is* able to reveal the murderer to you then at least you would be able to arrest and interrogate the guilty man and perhaps you would be able to convict him with other evidence."

"Indeed, Doctor, I suppose that may be a possibility. But now let us stop hypothesising and apply what we know about blackmailers and extortionists from cold, hard experience. This man has not contacted you because of his concern for justice and the public good. He wrote to you purely out of greed. He wants money and that is his prime motivation. I will concede that his letter is most unusual and well phrased to seem as if he is only asking for money because of his rank misfortune. But quite frankly, I don't believe him. He is a criminal, plain and simple. Furthermore, I strongly believe that *if* we were to pay him the £300,000 he is demanding then the next communication we receive from him will inform us that since we have paid the money so easily, he now considers that he has seriously underestimated the true value of his information. That being the case, if we truly want him to reveal the killer, it will cost yet more money. Possibly even yet another £300,000 and if we refuse to pay it then the first payment will be forfeit. And, of course, should the killer strike again it will be entirely our fault and *not* his! I'm afraid, sir, that that is how extortionists operate."

Dr. Pullman still looked doubtful. "I know that you are in a difficult position, Inspector Randan. What happens now?"

"You must complete your paperwork, sir. When do you think you can schedule the inquests?"

"I can release the bodies for burial forthwith. I think then we must try and see if we can identify some family or next of kin. As regards the inquests, I think it best in the circumstances if we open both inquests and then adjourn them immediately until your investigation is complete, one way or another."

"That does sound sensible, Doctor and I will inform the Commissioner of those facts when I report to him."

"You are going to report directly to Sir Edward Bradford?"

"That is correct Sir. He has asked me to keep him fully informed and whether O'Brien is paid the money, the decision will be his. Or perhaps it may even be made by those above him."

Pullman's eyebrows raised in amazement "Really? The Home Secretary? I find that incredible. Who could have imagined that the murder of a couple of prostitutes would draw such attention?"

"I really can't comment, sir. However, after the Whitechapel Murders we can see how easily a murderer can seize the attention of the press and the public in a way that draws even our political masters into the resulting entanglement."

"I will keep you informed, Inspector."

"Thank you, sir. I appreciate that."

Randan left the coroner's office and decided to walk back to Westminster in the hope that the autumn breeze would clear his lungs and his clothes of at least some of the stench of the mortuary. No matter how many times he had visited them, and he had visited more than a few over the years, he knew he would never get used to *that* smell.

When he reached the entrance of the Savoy Grill he was met by the ever-present Joseph. "Welcome, Inspector. Lady Meux told me you were coming here and she suggested that you might wish to make use of our eau de cologne in the washrooms. May I accompany you, sir?"

When Randan finally joined Valerie and Joan in their booth, Valerie couldn't help but smile at him. "My, my, Peter, I haven't smelt cologne that strong since my days working at the Casino!"

"Thank you, Valerie. I thought you might be more interested in my visit to Southwark?"

"Oh, don't be upset Peter. I'm only teasing. Besides, I already know what the coroner told you. Both Nellie and Matilda were murdered, were they not?"

"Yes, by the administration of strychnine poison. But you needn't look so smug. Unfortunately, we are no closer to knowing the identity of their murderer."

As Randan sat down with a pot of tea, Joseph appeared at the booth with the young sergeant who was temporarily running the Criminal Record Office. "Inspector Randan, this gentleman has asked to speak to you."

"Thank you, Joseph. Come in, Sergeant, You know Joan but this is Lady Valerie Meux who is assisting us in this inquiry." The sergeant stared open mouthed at Valerie. "Close your mouth, Sergeant and tell us why you are here, please."

Valerie smiled at the young police officer. "Don't be so rude, Peter. How can we help you, Sergeant?"

The sergeant pulled himself together "Sorry, ma'am. I did not mean to be rude or uncivil but I have come to warn Inspector Randan." The sergeant turned to speak directly to Randan. "You need to come back to the Yard right away, sir, the Commissioner is looking for you. And he seems to be in a state of … erm … severe agitation, sir!"

"Severe agitation, Sergeant?"

"Yes, exactly that, sir.

"Well, we can't have our Commissioner feeling severely

agitated, can we? I will come right away; your cup of tea will have to wait for another occasion."

Valerie interrupted "You definitely need me this time, Peter. I know how to handle Teddy, severely agitated or otherwise."

"Good Idea, Valerie. What about you, Joan?"

"I think the sergeant and I can go back to the office and get on with our work while you work on pacifying Sir Edward."

Robert Jeffries

Chapter Seven

Before going to his office, Inspector Randan collected the coroner's letter from the property office. Five minutes later, Randan and Valerie were standing outside Sir Edward Bradford's office door and despite Randan's lighthearted words to the sergeant, the fact that Valerie was beside him made him feel considerably less vulnerable.

The door opened and they were both ushered into the office where Commissioner Bradford sat unsmiling behind his desk. "Valerie, I wasn't really expecting you to be here, but now that you are, it's probably a good thing that you hear what has to be said. Now then, Randan, what on earth are you doing about this murder inquiry you are supposed to be dealing with? It won't do, you know, it simply will not do at all!"

Randan shuffled from one foot to the other. "I'm sorry, sir, I have no idea what you are talking about."

"Don't know what I'm talking about Randan? I'll tell you what I'm talking about and who is handling this investigation anyway? It seems to me that I know a damn sight more about it than you do! And it simply will not do at all, I tell you!" This was emphasised by the Commissioner thumping the desk with his fist.

Valerie broke in. "Now calm down, Teddy, this really isn't like you at all. Peter is doing a splendid job with his investigation and substantial progress has been made in a relatively short period of time. He has now established that the two women were definitely murdered by poisoning. Now, tell us why you are so upset?"

The Commissioner picked up a couple of envelopes and waved them across his desk. "These are why I am so upset Valerie and I could have told you that those two women were murdered. It says as much in these letters!"

The detective took hold of both letters and immediately saw that both envelopes contained handwritten sheets of paper. "With the greatest respect, sir, it will save a lot of time if you tell us what the contents of these envelopes are. Then I can read them for myself afterwards to see the full details."

Sir Edward took a deep breath and nodded in agreement. "The first envelope you have there is from Mr W.F.D. Smith. He has received a typed letter from someone called Doyle, accusing him of murdering the first girl with poison – Donworth, was it?"

Randan nodded at his senior officer "The other letter, sir? Who is that from?"

Sir Edward was still visibly flustered. "The second one is even worse. It is from Dr. William Broadbent. He received a typed letter from someone calling himself Malone. That letter accuses Dr. Broadbent of murdering the second woman, also by poisoning her!"

"Clover, Sir?"

"Yes, exactly. It's preposterous, absolutely unthinkable, completely out of the question!"

"I'm sorry, sir. Perhaps I have missed something? Why exactly are these allegations completely preposterous?"

"Randan, are you being serious? Isn't it obvious? Both these men are fine upstanding members of society and belong to the same clubs as I do. For them to be involved in sordid criminality of this type is absolutely unthinkable and such allegations as these are a vile slur against our entire society."

Valerie did her best to hide her smile, but Randan's face betrayed no emotion.

"Sir Edward, I'm afraid I don't recognise the names.

Can you tell me who they are?"

Again the Commissioner calmed himself. "Erm, yes, Mr Smith is the founder and owner of W.H. Smith, the stationers and booksellers and Dr. Broadbent is none other than the personal physician to Her Majesty Queen Victoria herself! What do you say to that, Randan?"

"I would ask another question, sir."

"Well, go on then, spit it out, man!"

"Did either or both of these letters also contain a demand for money to be paid to the writer in return for his silence?"

The Commissioner looked shaken again. "Yes, indeed. Both letters carried exactly that threat. How did you know that?"

Randan withdrew the coroner's letter from his jacket pocket and said, "Because it is all rather starting to fall into line with what we have in this letter, sir. This letter was addressed to Dr. Pullman, the Southwark Coroner appointed to investigate the deaths of Donworth and Clover. Ellen Donworth's initial autopsy proved inconclusive but Matilda Clover's death was originally put down to natural causes. This letter alleges that both women were in fact poisoned and the author claims that he knows the identity of the murderer and is willing to reveal that identity to the relevant authorities, providing he is first paid the sum of £300,000 for doing so."

The Commissioner suddenly seemed lost for words. "How much?"

"£300,000, sir"

"But that is completely absurd. We can never pay that sort of money!"

"Indeed, Sir Edward. I know it's not my decision, but my counsel would be that we should never pay any money to an extortionist, whether the sum demanded is £300,000 or £30. The chances of the blackmailer giving us any useful information are very slim."

"You think so?"

"I do, sir. I can't think of one single case where a ransom

has been paid and the desired result achieved."

"So we ignore it, then?"

"Oh, no, sir, certainly not that. We use the blackmailer's greed to draw him out and then arrest and charge him."

"Well, all that is very well Randan, but it won't get us any closer to arresting the actual murderer and surely that is what you are supposed to be concentrating on!"

"Once again, sir, I must respectfully disagree. When I came into your office, I had a great many thoughts regarding where this case might lead us, but these last few minutes have made everything much clearer in my mind. I now know who the murderer is."

"Really? Not Smith or Broadbent, I sincerely hope?"

At last Randan allowed himself a smile. "Indeed not, sir. Neither of those illustrious gentlemen are guilty of the murders of Ellen Donworth or Matilda Clover. The real murderer is none other than the person who sent the letters to Dr. Pullman at Southwark and to your acquaintances Mr. Smith and Dr. Broadbent. How else could he know so much about them? Find the writer of these letters and we also find the murderer."

"How do you propose to do that, Randan?"

"That's a very good question, sir and I am glad you asked it."

"Well, what is your plan?"

"When I think of one, sir, I promise I will let you know. Now, I must take these letters and read through them thoroughly as they may contain vital evidence."

The Commissioner at last seemed to have calmed down somewhat. "I have one clue for you straight away, Randan. I may not be a career detective, but I can spot the obvious when it is placed before me."

"Excellent, sir, and what might that be?"

"There is a common factor to all of these extortion letters, Randan."

"Quite so, sir, and that common factor is what, exactly?"

"Simple. The letter to the coroner was typed and Smith and Broadbent say in these letters that their blackmail letters

Poisonous City

were also compiled on typewriters. So there you have it, Randan! Typewriters! They are the tool of Satan himself and they are an abomination!"

Randan tried to conceal his look of surprise. "I beg your pardon, sir?"

At this point Valerie joined the conversation once again. "I think I see what Teddy is saying, Peter. Teddy is not an admirer of typewriters, are you, Teddy, dear?"

"No, Valerie, indeed I am not. They are infernal contraptions and they will not be used within the Metropolitan Police. At least, not while I am in charge of it."

Randan looked confused again. "Surely, sir, you can see that in some instances using a typewriter can increase efficiency, clarity and make for easier reading of documents?"

Sir Edward's eyes suddenly blazed brightly and Valerie took Randan by the arm. "Time to go, Peter. Teddy is a very busy man and we must let him get on with his work. See you soon, Teddy dear and Peter will keep you posted with his investigation."

Randan returned all the envelopes to his pockets as they both hurried out of Sir Edward's office.

"What was all that nonsense about typewriters, Valerie?"

"I would have thought Teddy made himself abundantly clear, Peter. He simply doesn't approve of them."

"Maybe so, Valerie, but to claim they are proof of murderous intent is ridiculous."

"Well, we all have our funny little ways and the world would be an infinitely duller place without our little eccentricities, wouldn't it? After all, I drive around town in carriages drawn by zebras. Some people actually seem to think that is unusual. Can you imagine that?"

Randan returned to his desk and examined the evidence. The typed letter addressed to the coroner was clearly evidence. The envelopes from Mr. Smith and Dr. Broadbent obtained from the Commissioner contained handwritten notes from both men clearly showing their shock and outrage at the blackmailer's allegations against them. Randan decided to keep them all together for evidential purposes. Both men would clearly have to be interviewed.

As he read through the letters from Mr. Smith and Dr. Broadbent, he gained the impression that these two men had entirely different personalities. Smith's letter seemed to contain almost a sense of humour with regards to the accusations. Dr. Broadbent, however, was clearly not at all amused by the letter that he had received.

After re-reading the letters, Randan was beginning to see a pattern developing. The letters from Smith and Broadbent confirmed that both extortion letters were typewritten and each purported to be sent by a person with a different name. He also imagined that neither of these letters would actually be signed. Just the same as the letter to Dr. Pullman. If this did indeed prove to be the case, then these very similarities could prove to be useful in identifying the murderer.

But first things first. He needed to speak to Mr. Smith and to Dr. Broadbent and find out if he could identify any possible link with each other or with the suspect, whoever that might be.

An hour later and the detective was walking from Bond Street Underground Station to Duke Street, Mayfair. He knocked on the front door of the address in his notebook. A few seconds later the door was opened by a liveried butler. Randan identified himself, produced his warrant card and asked to see Mr Smith. "Mr. Smith is actually expecting you, sir, please follow me."

Randan was admitted into a long hallway. The butler knocked on a large wooden door, opened it and announced, "Inspector Randan from New Scotland Yard is here to see you, sir."

"Excellent, please come in Inspector. I appreciate you coming so quickly. This is a very rum do indeed. It's not every day that one gets accused of murder!"

Randan looked at the smartly attired, middle-aged man sitting on the other side of his large oak desk and replied "I imagine not, sir. May I ask you first if you have kept the actual letter that was sent to you?"

"Why, yes, of course I have, I've read enough detective novels to know that original evidence is vital in catching these bounders." Mr Smith unlocked his desk drawer and produced the envelope containing his extortion letter and handed it to the detective.

Randan carefully removed the letter which was folded into quarters. As he expected, the letter was typed but unsigned. The name at the end of the letter was Doyle. Randan carefully read the letter. It was shorter than the letter sent to Dr. Pullman but he could immediately recognise the use of a similar style of prose. The letter stated that the author was in possession of clear evidence which linked Mr. Smith with Ellen Donworth and he could also prove that Mr Smith had tricked Donworth into taking a fatal dose of strychnine which resulted directly in her death. It went on to intimate that if such evidence were to be made public then the publicity alone would be enough to ruin his reputation and his business interests and if he wished to prevent that from occurring, then he must pay the writer the sum of £25,000 to ensure his silence. Failure to do so would result in his 'evidence' being made public. The blackmailer went on to state that he would be back in touch with Mr. Smith to arrange payment.

"This may seem a needless question, sir, but I must ask you. Do you have any idea who the author of this letter might be?"

"I'm afraid not Inspector, although If I were a betting man, I would wager a fair sum of money that Doyle is not his real name. Don't you think, Inspector?"

"Quite so, sir. I think it most unlikely. One other thing, sir, and I don't wish to sound indelicate, but once again, the question has to be asked."

"Don't worry, Inspector, I am fully aware that you have to do your job. You want to know if I have ever met or known this unfortunate lady he mentions, Donworth, I believe."

"That's correct, sir, Ellen Donworth. She was a victim of poisoning very recently in South London."

"I am very happy to be able to put your mind at rest there, Inspector. I have not been south of the river for quite some time and I have never, to my knowledge, met this poor woman."

"Thank you for clearing that up, sir. I will have to keep hold of this letter, as you correctly said. It is evidence in the case."

"I understand. I want to see this blackguard behind bars, Inspector. This is a terrible way to behave, trying to extort money from innocent people and from what the Commissioner told me in our communications, I am not the only victim. Can you tell me who else he has tried to implicate?"

"I'm afraid I cannot provide any further information at this stage, sir, but I can tell you that when this man does end up behind bars it may only be for a short period of time because I suspect his final destiny will be to fulfil an appointment with the hangman."

"For extortion and blackmail?"

"No, sir, for murder. If I am correct, then the person who wrote this letter to you is in fact the real murderer of Ellen Donworth and this letter may form part of the evidence that will, in time prove his guilt to a judge and jury. Now, before I leave, sir, I would like to take a very short witness statement from you relating to those questions I just asked you, will that be all right?"

"Of course, Inspector."

Randan wrote the required statement in his pocketbook and then read it back to the businessman. "Do you agree with that, sir?"

"Yes, it sounds fine."

"Very well, sir. Would you just sign and date it after the last word, please? "

"In that case, Inspector Randan, I wish you luck with your investigation.

Randan scribbled a few extra notes in his pocketbook

and then handed the book to Smith. "If you wouldn't mind signing this, sir. It's simply a receipt for your letter.

Smith glanced at the page and signed and dated the entry.

"Thank you, sir. I will see myself out."

Randan walked along Duke Street and crossed over Oxford Street. His next destination would be only a few minutes away. Dr. William Broadbent's consulting rooms were located in Harley Street. Randan checked the address in his notebook and five minutes later he was knocking on the large black door bearing the brass plate proclaiming that here worked and resided Dr. William Broadbent FRCS.

Once again Randan produced his warrant card as identification and once again he was informed that the doctor was expecting him.

Broadbent was a large imposing man with a bushy black beard and sideburns that were greying at his temples. "I hope this won't take long, Inspector. I have important patients to attend to."

Randan did not appreciate having limits imposed on his time by the people he was, after all trying to assist. "I shall be as quick as I can, sir, but as you told the Commissioner himself, this is a very serious matter."

"What exactly can I do for you, Inspector Randan?"

"The letter that you received, Doctor. May I see it, please?"

The progress of the meeting was almost exactly the same as his previous meeting with Mr Smith, but the Doctor's tone and general demeanour were not as polite as Mr. Smith's had been and he certainly did not have Mr. Smith's sense of humour.

Broadbent produced his letter and handed it to the detective, saying, "To be quite frank, Inspector. I resent the fact that you feel you have the need to come and interview me at all. Surely it must be patently obvious to any fool that the allegations made in this letter are a complete fabrication and you should be treating them as such."

Randan's expression remained completely unchanged as

he read the contents of the envelope which were almost a direct copy of the letter addressed to Mr. Smith. The only difference was that Dr. Broadbent was being accused of the murder of Matilda Clover and his letter purported to come from a man named Malone. "Since you are in such a rush Doctor, I will ask you just two questions and then I will be on my way. Firstly, do you have any idea at all who may have sent you this letter?"

Broadbent simply snorted. "None at all."

"And have you ever, to your knowledge, met the woman referred to in the letter?"

Broadbent looked as if he was about to explode in a fit of rage. "What type of man do you think I am, Inspector? I most certainly do not consort with common prostitutes, and I resent your tone and question! You may be assured that I will be reporting your impertinence to the Commissioner!"

Again, Randan's face betrayed no trace of emotion. "Thank you, sir. I will take that as a 'no' and by the way, who said anything about Miss Clover being a common prostitute?"

Broadbent's expression was like thunder. "I checked with the Southwark Coroner and he told me, damn you!"

The detective scribed the same statement in his pocketbook and read it out to the still fuming Doctor. " Do you agree with that, Doctor?"

"Yes, I suppose so."

"And I will need to keep this letter, sir. It's evidence."

Again, Broadbent sullenly signed the receipt. "Is that it, Inspector? Have you quite finished, or do you have any further stupid and inane questions that you wish to insult me with?"

"Not for now, sir, but if I think of any more then I will come back and see you again."

As he turned and left the consulting room, he could sense Broadbent's angry stare burying itself into his back like a dagger and he smiled as he stepped back onto the pavement of Harley Street.

Back in his office, he examined all three letters together for the first time. There were so many similarities and he now felt sure that they were all composed by the same person. Common factors pertaining to all three letters were that they were all folded into quarters and they were all three unsigned. That fact did not particularly surprise him. The writer would know that if the letters were hand written, it might be proven by a graphologist that all three were penned by the same hand. It is very difficult to disguise one's handwriting and even a signature might provide damning evidence against the writer. He was also now certain that the person attempting to extort money from the Government, Smith and Dr Broadbent was also the real murderer of Ellen Donworth and Matilda Clover. All he had to do was prove it!

As he pondered over the letters, a messenger from New Scotland Yard's Back Hall entered the office. "Inspector Randan?"

"Yes."

"The Commissioner wants to see you right away, sir."

"Well, that didn't take long, did it?"

"Pardon, sir?"

"Nothing, lad. I will attend him directly."

The route from the Criminal Records Office to the Commissioner's private offices had now become familiar to him. He knocked on the door and was ushered in by Sir Edward's secretary. "The Commissioner will see you right away, Inspector."

Randan stepped into the room and stood before his senior officer who was writing at his desk. "Ah. Randan. Can't you ever do anything without upsetting people? I have just had a message from Dr. Broadbent and he is furious about your visit to him this morning. He claims you were rude and impertinent and also that you accused him of consorting with common prostitutes! What have you got to say for yourself?"

"I wouldn't have quite put it like that, sir, but I think it is fair to say that we didn't exactly get on well together."

"From the tone of his message I would say that you were quite a long way from getting on well together, as you put it!

Damn it all man - he is the Queen's personal physician; couldn't you at least have tried to humour the pompous old fool?"

"I did try, sir – honestly!"

"All right, I am hereby giving you an official dressing down for being disrespectful to Dr. Broadbent. Now, did you gain any useful information from the idiot?"

"Nothing that I wasn't expecting, Sir Edward, but I am now convinced that we are working along the right lines." Randan produced all three letters from his inside jacket pocket and placed them on the desk. "This is the letter I showed you the other day, sir. The one that was sent to the Southwark Coroner demanding £300,000 for revealing the killer. The second letter is the one sent to Mr. Smith accusing him of killing Ellen Donworth and the third letter is the one sent to Dr Broadbent."

"Accusing him of killing Clover?"

"Exactly right, sir, and in both these letters the author is demanding the sum of £25,000 from Smith and Broadbent. I believe they were all written by the same person, although he uses a different identity in each instance."

"But we have no way of proving that, Inspector! This is one of the reasons why I detest typewriters. If the letters were hand written then we could instantly spot they were all written by the same hand. But you can't say that for certain about letters typed on a machine. This only proves my point!"

"If you will forgive me, sir, it proves no such thing. However, I believe that our suspect thinks as you do, that one letter composed on a typewriter is indistinguishable from any other similarly typed letter."

"Yes! That is precisely the case – isn't it?"

"No, sir, that is not the case at all." Randan rejoined. "I have recently been doing some research and I have read reports that suggest exactly the opposite. If you were to type something onto a piece of paper and then use another machine to type exactly the same thing onto another piece of paper, I believe that it would be possible for an expert to forensically examine both machines and both pieces of writing and then be able to prove which machine was used to type each example. It seems, sir, that the very mechanical nature of these machines makes them all very different from each other. The differences might be very subtle but they exist. It is rather like similar work that is being carried out on fingerprints. I think you have most certainly heard about that work, haven't you, sir?"

Sir Edward looked uncertainly at the detective. "Erm, yes, of course I have, but it's all very new and experimental, isn't it? I must confess that I'm not sure that I approve of all these modern ideas."

Again, Randan smiled at his senior. "Modern or not, sir we in the police must move on and keep up to date with new inventions and innovations if we are going to stay ahead of the criminals we are up against. The experts seem to think that there are no two fingerprints in the world that are identical. I do believe that one day we will compile a library of criminals' fingerprints and they will eventually be accepted as prima facie evidence in courts of law all around the world."

"Well, it won't be in my lifetime, Randan and anyway, we aren't talking about fingerprints, we are discussing typewriters, a very different kettle of fish entirely. You would need to prove that no two typewriters can produce identical results. Can you do that?"

"Not yet, sir, but I will work on it!"

With that, Randan picked up the three letters and made to leave the office.

"Just one second, Randan. You believe firmly that our killer and our letter writer are one and the same. Yes?"

"I do, sir."

"Well, if he genuinely expects to get away with murder and extortion and make money out of it, he must be insane or stupid, don't you think?"

Randan looked back across the Commissioner's desk and thought for a second. "I think we must be extremely wary about prejudging our murderer, sir. It may well be that the balance of his mind is disturbed and he may well possibly be clinically insane. But that does not at all mean that he is 'stupid' and I believe that to imagine him as such will be a grave error on our part. Judging from all the evidence we now have in our possession, I think I can draw a profile of our killer."

"Go on. What does this 'profile' look like?"

"I believe that our killer is a well-spoken, well educated, smartly dressed and possibly even handsome male, possibly with American or Canadian connections. I think he will have at the very least a knowledge of medicines and pharmaceuticals. I also think he will appear to his victims as polite, genuine and plausible. All of these attributes make him a formidable adversary, sir. Nothing in that profile suggests to me that he is stupid. Cunning, devious, greedy and highly dangerous, most certainly, but not, in my opinion, stupid, sir."

"Thank you, Randan. You had better crack on and catch him then!"

"Once again, sir, I will do my very best."

Chapter Eight

Randan returned to his desk in the Criminal Records Office on Wednesday morning with the intention of continuing his inspection of the letters but as he entered he was called over by the sergeant charged with running the office in his absence.

"Inspector Randan, your colleague, Lady Meux was here a short time ago looking for you. She seemed most … erm …"

"Agitated, Sergeant? It seems to be catching!"

"No, sir, I would say she was more excited than agitated. She said she and Joan would be at the Savoy Grill. Whatever it is, sir, I think she wants to tell you about it herself."

"I see, Sergeant, then I had better get over there right away and see what all the fuss is about. One should never keep a lady waiting."

Ten minutes later, Joseph was showing the detective into Valerie's private booth.

"Peter, where on earth have you been? Something important has turned up. This could be *really* important!"

"Very well, what has happened?"

"I will let Rose tell you."

For the first time, Randan noticed that Valerie's close friend Rose was also sitting in the booth.

"Hello Rose, tell me what has happened."

"It was last night, Inspector. I was holding one of our

group meetings in Lambeth. Everything was quite normal, and I had already spoken to four of our regular ladies but as I was preparing to leave our meeting room in the coffee house and head off home, another lady came in. She isn't really one of our regulars, but she does occasionally pop in, and we never turn anyone away who is genuinely seeking help. I asked her if she had had any success in giving up working on the streets. She'd told me that she had been trying very hard to leave the streets behind her and get a respectable job, as she called it but that when times were hard and money was really short then she was forced to go back to the streets, looking for punters. It really is not an unusual story. Then I asked her if she was in a stable relationship with anyone. I know from past meetings with her that she used to be in a relationship with a casual labourer but that relationship could sometimes turn violent, especially if they had been drinking. She told me that her relationship with that man had ended but that she had met another man who treated her much better and that she held high hopes that they might even have a future together. I told her that this all sounded very encouraging and I asked her what he was like. She told me that although she had first met him in a working capacity, he was a real gentleman and was very polite and respectable. Then she told me that he spoke with an American accent and that he was a qualified doctor. That was when alarm bells started ringing in my mind. It all sounded very much like the same man that Ellen Donworth had mentioned before she died! I asked her if this man had ever offered her any drinks or perhaps any medication. She said that he had not but that he had said that he would like them to go out somewhere together and see more of each other."

Randan was listening intently. "Did you warn her about this man?"

"Yes, of course, I thought it was the only sensible thing to do, but she wasn't at all happy. I think she may have thought that I was just trying to spoil things for her. Maybe even steal him for myself. But I think I succeeded in getting through to her that she needed to protect herself and take the greatest of care."

"Good, well done, Rose. Do we have an address for this lady?"

"No, but I do have a contact address for a very good friend of hers and they are often in each other's company."

"Excellent, what is this lady's name, Rose?"

"Her name is Hazel Peters."

"Then we need to make contact with her friend without delay. You were quite right Valerie. This could indeed be a significant development and we have no time to lose."

Valerie and Rose both had a worried expression on their faces. Valerie spoke first. "Peter, I cannot stress strongly enough that we must proceed with caution here or we risk ruining all the hard work that Rose and I have done over the last few years with these women. They do not view police officers as their friends and we must think very carefully about how we are going to proceed with these two ladies before we go to them. We must agree on a plan and then stick with it."

Randan looked at both Valerie and Rose. "Very well, how do you think we should proceed?"

Valerie thought for a second or two. "Rose, who is this friend of Hazel Peters?"

"Her name is Lizzie Collins and she lives in a room in a tenement block in Dean's Court, close to the Doulton china works. I don't know the full address but I can take us there."

"I have a proposal," said Randan. "Why don't we let Rose take us all to where Lizzie Collins lives. Joan and I can wait outside while you both speak to her and impress on her the urgency of why I need to speak to Hazel. She needs to know that we don't intend to harm Hazel in any way. Indeed we may possibly be able to prevent her being yet another murder victim. Does that make sense?"

Valerie and Rose both nodded agreement and fifteen minutes after leaving the Savoy Grill the four of them were walking quickly across the down-river footway of Westminster Bridge. Once across the bridge they dodged the busy horse drawn traffic as they crossed the road and descended the steps leading onto the Albert Embankment. They continued past St

Thomas' Hospital and then past Lambeth Palace. Rose led them across the road that took them onto Lambeth Bridge and past White Hart Dock where the clay barges bound for the Doulton factory were unloaded. Just past Broad Street, Rose led them down a small, unnamed alleyway with ugly, dark tenement blocks on either side of the narrow lane. For a second Rose seemed confused but she quickly regained her bearings and pointed to one particular block. "This is the one. Lizzie has a room on the third floor."

Valerie and Rose disappeared into the dark and forbidding tenement block, their smart dresses looking very much out of place in the dirt and squalor of the area. Ten minutes later they reappeared in the company of a small, undernourished female in drab clothes with untidy, unwashed hair of indeterminate colour.

Rose spoke first. "These are the two people from New Scotland Yard that we told you about in your room, Lizzie. They are not here to cause trouble for either you or Hazel, but we all think that Hazel might be in great danger from the new gentleman that she has grown so fond of. This officer needs to ask her a few questions about him."

The woman answered in a coarse South London accent. "You think that this bloke is the same geezer what topped poor Nellie and Matilda, dontcha?"

"It is a possibility, but we need to find out for certain," Randan replied.

"She ain't gonna thank ya none, y'know? Proper stuck on this Yank geezer she is. She finks that 'ee's 'er ticket out of this shit'ole. I've tried to tell 'er that 'es just like all the rest but she won't 'ave none of it! She's got a romantic streak in 'er that one 'as and that's the truth."

"Well, perhaps she's right. We just want to check this man out. If he is genuine then we can look elsewhere. I just want you and Hazel to understand that we are not here to make life harder for either of you. If she is wrong and we are correct, then Hazel may well be in very great danger."

"Yeah? Well good luck with explaining that to 'Azel, copper, but she is a mate o' mine and I don't wanna see no 'arm come to her, so I will 'elp you out. But you just mind that you keep straight with us. Miss Valerie an' Miss Rose have done good work round 'ere. If you ain't being straight about this nobody will trust 'em ever again. So you better be on the level."

"We understand, Miss Collins; where can we find Hazel?"

Lizzie laughed out loud. "Nobody ain't never called me 'Miss Collins' before an' you will never find 'er, copper. This place is closed to the likes of you. I will take you to 'er and me and Miss Rose 'ere might just be able to persuade 'er that you is on the straight and narrer and if we can do that then per'aps she might agree to talk to you's. But I ain't making no promises. D'ya 'ear me?"

"Perfectly," replied the detective.

Randan, Joan, Valerie and Rose followed Lizzie Collins through the winding alleyways and streets of Lambeth. At last they arrived at another unnamed close that contained several shabby tenement buildings very similar to the ones where they had found Lizzie.

"'Azel lives in 'ere," said Lizzie "Yous three had better wait 'ere while me and Miss Rose goes and 'as a chat with 'er. With a bit of luck we might be able to get 'er to come out and speak to you but she won't speak with you out 'ere in the street. The people round 'ere can smell a copper a mile off an she won't wanna be seen talking to the likes of yous in public, so we'll 'ave to go somewhere else."

"Do you know of anywhere suitable?" asked Randan.

"Yeah, maybe the little coffee house where Miss Rose and Miss Valerie meets with us working girls. That should be fine and it's close enough."

Rose agreed "Yes, that's where I spoke with Hazel yesterday. I'm not sure how she will react to seeing me again though. She was quite angry with me when she left yesterday. Perhaps Valerie should go with Lizzie?"

Valerie looked doubtful. "I've only met her very briefly a couple of times. You know her better than I do, Rose."

Lizzie finally settled the matter. "I think Miss Rose will

be all right, She'll be with me and me and 'Azel go back a long way."

Randan glanced across at Rose and Valerie and they both nodded assent. "Very well. Are you sure you are all right going in alone, Rose?"

"Yes, of course, Inspector. I'll be fine with Lizzie."

Rose followed Lizzie into the dark lobby of the tenement block.

"I'm not at all happy about letting her go in alone, Valerie. Not happy at all."

"She is a tough woman, Peter. Don't forget our backgrounds, Rose can look after herself."

However, Randan caught the tension in her voice and knew that for all her positivity, Valerie shared at least some of his misgivings. He kept checking his pocket watch and after twenty minutes had elapsed, he became increasingly agitated. "If they aren't out within the next couple of minutes, I'm going in to look for them. I should have known better than to put Rose in danger."

As soon as he had spoken the words, Valerie's attention was drawn to a sound above her head. They both looked up to see Rose waving to them from a second-floor landing. "Sorry for the delay, we are coming down now."

A short while later, Rose and Lizzie emerged from the darkness with a small, slight woman, Randan guessed from her appearance that she might have been in her late twenties or early thirties. Her attire was neat but worn. The expression on her face was one of deep displeasure.

"This is 'Azel," said Lizzie. "I've told 'er what all this 'ere is about and at first she didn't want nuffink to do with yous. But, Miss Rose an I 'ave told her that she ain't in no trouble with the law and yous just wanna have a word with 'er about 'er new geezer and we can do that all at the coffee house."

The group walked in silence until they reached the small coffee house where Rose and Valerie conducted their meetings. They all sat round a couple of tables in the otherwise deserted room and Hazel spoke for the first time.

Her accent was local but her tone and delivery was not as coarse as that of Lizzie.

"Tell me what all this is about."

The policeman introduced himself and showed his warrant card. "I am Inspector Randan of New Scotland Yard and I am investigating two murders."

Hazel interjected. "Nellie Donworth and Tilda Clover? I've heard they were killed. But that ain't got nothing to do with me, I swear it ain't."

"I can assure you that you are not a suspect in the deaths of Miss Donworth or Miss Clover but we understand that you have recently met a gentleman and we wish to speak to him so that we can eliminate him from our inquiries."

"You mean Freddy? No! You are wrong! He can't possibly have anything to do with those murders. He's a good man and you are completely wrong, I know it!"

The detective's voice remained soft and measured. "I sincerely hope you are right, Hazel and if you are, then we will leave you alone and not bother you again. However, if the man you know as Freddy is the man we are looking for, then you may be in very grave danger."

"How can you tell for sure whether it is or isn't him?"

Randan indicated Valerie. "Ellen Donworth was one of the ladies that Miss Rose and Miss Valerie here have been trying to help to improve their circumstances. Ellen met Valerie here shortly before she died. During the meeting Ellen was clearly unwell but believed herself to be suffering from a bad cold or something similar. During their conversation, Ellen spoke to her about a new man that she had recently met who she considered to be a gentleman and whom she hoped might take her out of her life on the streets. Shortly after that meeting, Miss Valerie found out that Ellen was dead. As you are already aware, shortly after Ellen Donworth's death, Matilda Clover also died in unusual circumstances. That is when Miss Valerie sought to enlist my assistance. My inquiries have revealed that both women were poisoned.

"But that's got nothing to do with my Freddy, I'm

positive about that."

"I sincerely hope not, but during her final interview with Ellen, Miss Valerie asked her about this new man in her life and Ellen described him quite well. All we want to do is find out if Ellen's description of her man might possibly also fit the description of your Freddy."

Hazel looked nervous but resolute "You tell me how Nellie described her man and I will tell you if it sounds like Freddy. Will that do you?"

Randan smiled, "I have a slightly different way of doing this Miss Peters, please bear with me. Can I ask you to describe Freddy to me, starting with his physical appearance?"

"He is tall, slim and dark haired. He has a moustache, and he's quite handsome, I think."

"How does he dress, Hazel?"

"He is always very smart, sometimes he will wear evening dress and a top hat that makes him look even taller."

"How does he speak?

"He is very correct and refined, I would say. He is always very polite and kind to me. That's how I know he just can't be your murderer."

"You said that his accent is 'refined'? Does he have an English accent?"

"No, absolutely not. If anything his accent was either American or Canadian, I think, but that might be because he told me he has spent some years over there."

"I see, what about his eyes? Do you know what colour they are?"

"Not really. I didn't really like to stare at his eyes too much. I thought he might think I was rude."

"Why would he think that, Hazel?"

"Because sometimes I could see that he had a considerable squint, and he looked a bit cross eyed."

"Does he ever speak about his work?"

"Not about his work in London, in fact I don't think he is currently working, though he did say that in America, he was trained in medicine and had even qualified as a doctor.

He is very clever."

"Quite. Has he ever offered you any tablets or medicines?"

"No, definitely not, there's no need to. I am very healthy, as you can see."

"What about his sense of humour, Hazel? Would you say that he was serious and stern, perhaps sometimes a little frightening?"

Hazel relaxed a little. "Oh, not at all, not my Freddy. He is always laughing and joking."

"One last question, Hazel. You say that he is always laughing? When he laughs, does his voice sometimes go up very high so that it sounds as if it is almost a screech?"

Hazel looked shocked "How could you possibly know that, copper?"

The detective looked directly at Hazel. "Because that is exactly how Nellie Donworth described her gentleman friend the day after he had given her what proved to be a lethal dose of strychnine."

"Oh, dear God. No! It can't be Freddy. You're lying to me!"

"I'm afraid it's the truth, Miss Peters. How else could we have known about his unusual laugh? And I'm afraid the rest of your description fits our suspect too. I believe you have had a very fortunate escape. I strongly suspect that he intended you to be his next victim."

Valerie interjected, "I really am so sorry that you had to find out this way, Hazel but now we must catch this man you know as Freddy before he kills anyone else. Do you know where he lives?"

Hazel dabbed the tears on her cheek with a handkerchief. "It's all right, I'm fine. I should have known that he was too good to be true. The likes of me ain't supposed to find happiness. I can't tell you where he lives. But I will help you catch the bastard, if I can. An' that's a promise."

"Hazel, if he contacts you again we must know about it. How do you usually meet?"

"He knows what streets I normally use when I'm working. He finds me."

"In that case, I need to watch you when you are out working and hope that he turns up."

"Friday nights are usually the night when he comes looking for me."

"In that case, this next Friday night is the night when you will have me in close attendance. Where do you normally look for clients, Hazel?"

"Lambeth Walk around the junction with Walnut Walk. I can't believe I am telling this to a bleedin' copper!"

"About what time?"

"I usually have a tot of gin in the pub on the corner at around eight then take up my position at about eight thirty. If he is going to turn up it will be between eight forty five and nine."

"I will be there, but out of sight."

Hazel gave a resigned grunt and just said, "I suppose so."

Lizzie said that she would take her friend back to her lodgings and Valerie, Rose, Randan and Joan headed back towards the Albert Embankment. "Do you think she really will help us find this man, Peter?" asked Valerie.

"I think so, Valerie, but we will find out for sure on Friday night."

"I will be with you, too."

"No, Valerie. I want to concentrate on Hazel and our suspect. Please trust me with this and *don't* go over my head to Sir Edward. I will let you know as soon as there is any definite news."

Chapter Nine

Randan walked into the Criminal Record Office at New Scotland Yard the following morning and was addressed by the sergeant who was filling in for him.

"Good morning, sir. How are your inquiries progressing?"

"They are going very well indeed, Sergeant. Indeed, I think we now have a suspect."

"Really? That is fast work, sir."

"Thank you. I was rather wondering if you might wish to be a little further involved in the investigation, Sergeant and maybe get involved in some actual police work rather than sitting behind this desk all day?"

"Nothing would please me more, sir! What do you have in mind?"

Randan recounted his meeting with Hazel Peters the previous afternoon and explained that he planned to keep observation on Hazel as she worked her usual ground in Lambeth Walk the following night.

"Can I ask what you plan to do if your suspect puts in an appearance, sir?"

"Most certainly, Sergeant. I fully intend to ruin his night by taking him to Lambeth Police Station and interrogating him regarding the deaths of Donworth and Clover."

"Won't that tip him off that you know what he is up to,? Do you think you have enough evidence against him to charge him with the murders?"

"No, Sergeant, I fear that I don't as yet have sufficient evidence to lay a charge against this man, but I do have sufficient evidence which leads me to strongly suspect that he is at least in some way involved in both murders and that gives me ample grounds to arrest him on suspicion of his involvement in both felonies. Once he is safely in custody, we will be able to find out a great deal more about him."

"Such as, sir?"

"His name, for one thing. I think he uses a variety of aliases every time he commits an offence, doubtless in an attempt to confuse suspicious police officers. Once we know his real name, perhaps our inquiries will turn up even more criminal activity."

"Where and when shall we meet tomorrow, sir?"

"I think here in this office tomorrow evening at seven, Sergeant. Then we can make our way to Lambeth Walk and find a suitable location that gives us a good view of the junction with Walnut Walk. Then it will just be a matter of waiting."

"Will you make yourself known to Hazel Peters beforehand, sir? "

"No, I think not. I told her yesterday that I would be in the vicinity tomorrow night. But I don't really want to give her the opportunity of changing her mind as regards assisting the investigation. We will just make our observation as discreet as possible and see what happens. If a man who fits the description appears, then we will step in."

"Are you expecting any resistance if we do approach him, sir?"

"I would not have thought so, Sergeant, but I think we should both be carrying our truncheons and whistles just in case."

"Right you are, sir. I'll see you here tomorrow at seven in the evening."

Randan turned to leave the office but then checked and turned again to face the sergeant. "I'm sorry, Sergeant, I have no idea of your name; what is it?"

"Parry, sir. Nathaniel Parry. But people normally call me Nathan."

"Excellent; my name is Peter. It has been some considerable time since I did any surveillance work but I doubt if too much has changed and it might just make us stand out to the good people of Lambeth if we keep calling each other sir, sergeant or inspector. So for the purpose of tomorrow, I will call you Nathan and you should call me Peter.

Nathan smiled at his senior officer, "That's a good idea, Peter."

Randan half frowned "Don't get carried away, Sergeant," but then grinned at his new partner as he left the office.

The following day, Randan arrived at New Scotland Yard at precisely six forty-five and found Nathan Parry ready to go. "Cup of tea before we go, sir? There's no telling how long we'll be out there."

"Good idea, we have time."

The two men sat quietly and sipped their cups of tea. "Do you think our suspect will show up tonight, sir?"

Randan shrugged, "I have no way of being sure but I hope he does. I'm keen to put a face to our killer and extortionist and Hazel Peters seemed confident that he would put in an appearance."

"You think we can trust her then?"

"I do. I wasn't convinced when we first met her but when she realised that she had been lied to and misled by this man, she definitely turned against him. I suppose there are very few things in life as sobering as suddenly realising that you have just narrowly escaped becoming the next victim of a murderer. Now, let's go and find our suspect."

The two officers walked along the Victoria Embankment towards Westminster Bridge and then crossed over the bridge before turning right and walking along the Albert Embankment towards Lambeth Bridge. They reached Lambeth Walk via Lambeth Road and Lollard St. They arrived at the junction of Lambeth Walk and Walnut Walk at seven fifty and looked around for a good vantage point that would provide a clear view of the junction.

"By the way," said Nathan. "I decided to call in a favour from an old friend of mine on 'L' Division. He is a sergeant at Lambeth and I asked him to have a constable with a handcart standing by close to the location but out of eyesight between eight thirty and ten just in case we need some extra assistance. If we need him, we just have to blow a whistle."

"Let's just hope he stays hidden until we need him. Something else I am hoping for is that Hazel is sensible enough not to walk around too much. I really don't want to keep changing our position in order to keep her in view."

They finally settled themselves in an alcove which contained the entrance to a pawnbroker's shop that had closed its doors and secured its shutters for the night. This vantage point provided them with the opportunity of being able to observe the junction which was a little over fifty yards distant but it also meant that they could duck back out of view if they needed to.

"This spot should suit us admirably, Nathan" said Randan and the sergeant nodded his agreement. "Now, we wait."

At eight, Randan glanced at his pocket watch. "Hazel should be in the public house by now. I hope she doesn't have too much to drink. I really do need her to be sober if he turns up."

Slightly after eight thirty Randan tensed slightly. "There she is, Nathan. She is the woman in the green dress and the yellow bonnet."

"Are you sure? I can't make out her face from here."

"I'm positive. She has a distinctive way of standing and walking. That's her and she is right on time."

The two men observed Hazel closely. She approached and spoke to a number of men in the next ten minutes but the contact with all of them was brief.

"It looks as if she is trying to work, Peter. If she picks up a client, it will ruin everything!"

"On the other hand" said Randan, "If our suspect is also watching her, and she is obviously not trying to earn her money, then that might alert him that something is wrong. Let's just see what happens."

Just before nine, a tall and well-dressed gentleman wearing a black frock coat and a tall top hat appeared from around a corner and made his way towards Hazel. As he approached the woman, they could faintly hear him calling to her in a friendly manner.

"Nathan, this could be our man."

"Shall we make a move now?"

"No. Not just yet."

The tall stranger reached out towards Hazel and she greeted him warmly then kissed him on both cheeks.

Nathan smiled "Do you think that was for our benefit? Betrayed by a kiss? It's all rather biblical."

"I don't really care, Nathan, but now I think it's time to go and have words with our friend. By the way, don't say anything to Hazel. If she has any sense she will drift away as soon as we identify ourselves."

The two officers walked quickly towards the junction and as they approached from behind, the stranger was unaware of their presence until Randan took his man by the elbow and announced, "I am Inspector Randan of New Scotland Yard and I wish to talk to you with regard to the murders of Ellen Donworth and Matilda Clover".

As soon as Randan showed his warrant card, Hazel melted away into the background exactly as he had hoped she would.

The suspect seemed momentarily stunned and lost for words but quickly recovered his poise and replied in an educated transatlantic accent, "You wish to talk to me about two murders? I can assure you that I have not the remotest idea what you might be talking about. I know absolutely nothing about any murders and I have never heard of those women. You are making a serious mistake here and I must ask you to remove your hand from my arm."

Randan retained his hold on his suspect's arm. "If that is

indeed the case then you will be released as soon as possible and with my sincere apologies. However, until I have made my inquiries, you are going nowhere."

"This is completely preposterous, and you have an innocent man here. I demand that you release me." As he completed the sentence his voice rose almost to a high-pitched squeal, a fact that was not missed by the detectives.

Randan spoke forcefully. "You will accompany us quietly and willingly to Lambeth Police Station where I will question you regarding these murders and some other connected offences. If, however, you refuse to do this willingly, then I will arrest you forthwith and you will be taken there, by force if necessary."

"You can go to hell, copper. I am going nowhere with you. Now, unhand me immediately."

Randan signalled to Nathan. "The whistle please, Sergeant."

Nathan removed his police whistle from his coat pocket and blew three shrill blasts. Within thirty seconds a couple of burly Lambeth police constables appeared from around the corner pushing a hand cart.

Randan addressed his suspect again. "Very well, you have made your choice. I am arresting you on suspicion of murder. You can walk the short distance to the police station like a gentleman or we will strap you into that cart and push you there. Which will it be?"

The stranger stuttered, "I have never been so insulted in all my life. I will have your badges for this outrage. You have no idea who you are talking to."

"Strap him in, gentlemen!"

As the officers moved menacingly towards the suspect, he suddenly relented. "All right, *stop*! I will walk with you to the police station but I can assure you that all of you will bitterly regret this ridiculous insult."

The two Lambeth pc's stood down reluctantly but followed the small party to Lambeth Police Station, just in case.

The two detectives walked either side of their newly

arrested prisoner during the short walk to Lambeth Police Station. They entered the station yard by the rear gate and went into the building through a heavy door. The charge room was on the ground floor. Randan entered first followed by his increasingly sullen prisoner and Parry followed behind. He closed the charge room door behind them once they were all inside, having already thanked and dismissed the two Lambeth officers.

Randan was pleased to see that the room was quiet and that the station officer was sitting at a desk while writing in a ledger. Randan showed his warrant card and identified himself to the station officer.

"May I ask what you have arrested this man for, sir?"

"On suspicion of murder, Sergeant."

"I see, sir. I think the duty officer should deal with this and I will inform him right away, sir."

A couple of minutes later, the sergeant returned with the duty officer who wore two stars on his tunic, denoting the rank of inspector.

"Inspector Randan?"

Randan acknowledged with a simple "Yes."

"May we speak outside, please?" He indicated a second door which led from the charge room to the station office.

Before the two officers could depart, the prisoner sprang to his feet and began speaking in a raised voice. "Are you the officer in charge here? I wish to make a serious complaint against these two officers who have taken away my liberty and accused me of a completely false and monstrous charge."

The duty officer stopped in mid-stride and turned towards the prisoner. "We will deal with your allegations in due course, sir, but first I want to speak to this officer and find out what this is all about. When I have done that, I will return here and we will proceed to take your details."

"You most certainly will not be taking my details, Inspector, because I have done absolutely nothing wrong. I demand that you release me forthwith or I will be forced to consider that you are in league with these two thugs and add your name to those I fully intend to complain about."

The inspector smiled at the prisoner. "As I said, sir, all in good time." He opened the adjoining door and ushered Randan through it. "Well, he certainly doesn't seem to be at all happy with you, Inspector Randan, does he?"

"So it would seem," replied the detective.

"Can I ask you how advanced your case is at this stage?"

"As yet I have no prima facie evidence against him but the circumstantial evidence I have uncovered is compelling and the deeper I look into this matter the more convinced I am that this prisoner is responsible for the recent murder of two women in Lambeth whose deaths I am investigating."

"Believing and proving are two very different things. Tell me what you've got thus far."

The two men sat in a side office and Randan recounted the events that followed the deaths of Ellen Donworth and Matilda Clover. At the end of the account, the duty officer remarked, "You're right, you really don't have any prima facie evidence, do you? And I have to tell you that could be a problem. The superintendent here is a stickler for the rules. He has eyes firmly fixed on attaining higher ranks and he is not a man to take risks by detaining prisoners overly long when there is little or no physical evidence linking them with a crime, particularly when they are loudly threatening complaints and possible legal action. What's your plan?"

"Originally, I planned to bring him in simply for questioning. However, he was having none of that and so I had to arrest him on suspicion. However, the fact that he is refusing to cooperate in any way, shape or form might just work in my favour!"

"How so?" asked the local inspector.

"When we return to the charge room we can start the process of booking him in. I suspect that he will refuse all details and make further dire threats against us. At that point I will tell him that if he refuses to tell us who he is and where he lives, we will detain him for as long as it takes for us to identify him ourselves. Then we search him and let him cool his heels in one of your cells. When we arrested him, it came as a complete surprise to him and I have been watching him very closely. He has not had any opportunity to rid himself of any possible evidence. I'm hoping that he will have identification on his person right now."

"One other thing, Inspector"

"What's that?"

"I believe this man has already killed twice in fairly quick succession. I further believe that if he is not stopped now then he will probably kill again. It is vital that we prevent him from doing that."

"Let's hope you are correct, then, Inspector Randan."

The two inspectors returned to the charge room and the duty officer addressed the prisoner.

"Now, sir, as you know you have been brought here on suspicion of being involved in murder and this officer wishes to ask you some questions regarding this matter. Before he can do that, I need to go through some basic procedures which involve getting your name and address and some other personal details. What is your name, please?"

The prisoner replied, "I have nothing to say."

"Come now, sir. This will not do you any good in the long run, you know? The longer you prevaricate the longer this procedure will take. If you really are, as you say, completely innocent of these allegations, then the best thing to do is to behave reasonably and answer the questions which should prove your innocence."

The prisoner grinned at the inspector. "Yes, I am quite sure that it would be the best thing *for you* if I complied with your wishes, but here's the thing, Inspector. I am a highly respected doctor in the United States and although I am not by any means an expert on English law, I do know some very basic things. Firstly, I know that policemen are the same all over the world and they will stop at nothing to prove their case. Little things like the innocence of the accused person must not get in the way of them gaining a conviction. Secondly, I know very well that it is the duty of the police to prove the guilt of the accused person, it is *not* incumbent to the accused to prove his innocence. I am completely innocent of any criminal act and I know for sure that you possess no hard evidence. I know this because there *is* no hard evidence against me! So you thugs do whatever you have to do, but I am not going to lift one finger to assist you." As he finished his address the prisoner was becoming increasingly excited in his speech and the final words were delivered almost in a screech.

The two inspectors glanced at each other and the duty officer continued, "Very well, sir. I have given you every opportunity to help yourself in this matter but your obstinacy leaves me with no other options. Gaoler! Come and assist these officers in searching this prisoner but remember you must use no more force than is required to successfully carry out the search. Then place him in a cell. Make sure you also remove his belt and shoelaces. I don't want him coming to any harm in my police station."

Then he addressed the prisoner again. "They are going to search your person. I will advise you not to obstruct them. Do you understand?"

"I understand perfectly Inspector and I will not resist. After all, I certainly would not want to accidentally fall down a flight of stairs and injure myself, would I?" Once again, the final word was delivered in a screech.

The two detectives and the gaoler thoroughly searched the prisoner, laid his property on the desk in front of him and the items were duly recorded in the ledger. At the end of the search, which was carried out in almost complete silence, the duty officer once again addressed the prisoner.

"This is a list of everything we have taken off you. If you agree with it, then I will ask you to sign immediately under the final item."

Once again the prisoner grinned. "Please don't take me for a fool, Inspector."

"Very well, take him down, gaoler and keep a regular watch on him. No longer than thirty minute intervals. Do you understand?"

The gaoler nodded and marched the prisoner into the cell block. He selected an empty cell, placed the prisoner inside and slammed the door behind him before double locking it and closing the small wicket hatch in the cell door. Before returning to the charge room, he wrote the words 'Male Anon, Murder' and 'Insp. Randan' on the adjacent chalkboard.

No sooner had the prisoner disappeared from view than Randan and Parry began examining the property that had just been removed from the suspect. Randan's hands moved straight to the pocket book and envelopes containing correspondence.

"I have a feeling, Sergeant Parry, that we are about to find out a great deal more about our suspect. In fact, I think we can at last put a name to him, this pocketbook is the property of Dr. Thomas Neill Cream and this correspondence is addressed to Dr. Cream at 103 Lambeth Palace Road."

Parry picked up a set of keys from the desk and smiled. "And I imagine that these keys will let us in; shall we go?"

Randan shook his head. "No, not yet, Sergeant. We must do this strictly by the book. Before we go to check his address, we will secure a search warrant. I don't want our hard-won evidence declared inadmissible because we have not followed proper procedure."

The duty officer smiled at the other two officers. "There speaks the voice of experience, Sergeant, but look lively you two. Once my superintendent finds out that we have this Yank in his cells he will be wanting to see some hard evidence to justify us detaining him in custody."

The duty officer looked up the name and address of the local justice of the peace and Randan and Parry were knocking on his front door within fifteen minutes of leaving the police station. The magistrate opened his front door to the two officers who, having identified themselves and showed their warrant cards, apologised for disturbing him at home and then explained why they were there.

Having listened to their request the magistrate confirmed that he was aware of the murders that had recently occurred. "What exactly are you hoping to find at this man's address in Lambeth Palace Road?" queried the magistrate.

Randan replied, "Since the suspect has been completely uncooperative with us, firstly I want to prove his address and identification. Then I will be looking for evidence relating to the offences that I believe he may have committed, particularly of course the murders but also anything possibly related to extortion letters that I believe he may also have sent."

The magistrate listened intently and commented, "This suspect of yours does not do anything by halves, does he?"

Randan replied, "It certainly does not appear so, sir."

The magistrate took a search warrant form from his drawer and filled in the relevant sections and eventually handed the warrant to Randan. "Gentlemen, if and when this man appears in court, I sincerely hope that it will be on a date when I am sitting and I wish you good luck with your inquiries."

With that the detectives were shown out and began to make their way to 103 Lambeth Palace Road.

When they arrived it was late and the building seemed dark and quiet. It was a three-storey building and Randan realised there must be many people living inside it.

"I think perhaps that the direct approach might be the best one to use here, Sergeant." He removed the prisoner's keys from his pocket and offered the large mortise key up to the lock on the front door and turned it. The key turned and the door swung open as he pushed it. As they stepped into the hallway they could both hear a bell tinkling in a ground floor room. After a few seconds, a door leading off the passageway swung open and light from the room lit the dark hallway. A small, scruffy and dishevelled middle-aged man emerged from the room and eyed the two detectives suspiciously.

"Who the 'ell are you and what do you want at this time of night?"

Once again Randan had his warrant card ready to prove his identity. "We have a search warrant to search this address with regard to a very serious matter. Are you the landlord here?"

"What if I am? Can't this all wait until the morning?"

"No, sir, it cannot wait until morning. As I just told you, these inquiries are of a very serious nature."

"Well, unless you can give me a bit more information as to what or who you are looking for, you will take a very long time executing your search warrant, Inspector. This is a big building."

"The rooms we are interested in are occupied by a man who claims to be a doctor. Do you have such a man residing here?"

"You don't mean that flash Yank, do you? He keeps telling me that he is a doctor but I've never seen him working. He dresses the part, though. Whenever he leaves here he dresses like he is setting off for Harley Street. He really dresses like a toff but I've always 'ad me doubts about him. I wouldn't trust him as far as I can spit. I've always 'ad him down as a wrong'un, do you know what I mean? What's he been up to anyway?"

"We can't reveal the exact nature of our investigation, but I would like to know what name he goes by here?"

"He calls himself Cream, Doctor Cream. I think I heard him say that his first name was Thomas. Is he the bloke you're after?"

"I think we can begin our inquiries with his rooms. Can you take us there, please?"

The scruffy man led the detectives up flights of winding stairs to the top floor.

"If you are going to break his door down, I'll be suing the old bill to pay for the damage, you mark my words!"

Randan produced keys once again. "I'm hoping that won't be necessary and that this second key should fit his door. Stand aside please." He offered the smaller key up to the round lock and turned it. Once again the key turned in the lock and the door swung open when he pushed it. "I'm pretty sure these are the rooms we are looking for, unless you know of any other rooms he uses in this building?"

"Nope. These are the only ones he uses here. I doubt if he could afford to rent any other rooms. These are the cheapest lodgings in the entire building. He dresses like a toff but he lives like a pauper. He's always late with his rent and he never has any cash. All his dressing up in fine clothes is just a front. The truth is, he ain't even got a pot to piss in!"

"Thank you for showing us this far. You can go now. We'll let ourselves out when we have finished."

The landlord turned away in a disappointed manner but then turned back to the detectives before leaving. "And when you see him next you can tell that flash Yank that he needs to start looking for other digs. This is a respectable establishment and I ain't 'aving the likes of him bringing my lodging house into disrepute. You make sure you tell him that! I *always* 'ad him down for a wrong 'un. Straight up, I did!"

Randan and Parry entered the room and turned up the gas lights. The two rooms were small, dark and dingy. Randan said, "Let's take one room each and see what we can turn up. When we have both finished, we can swap over just to double check that we haven't missed anything."

Parry nodded and headed into the bedroom. Both officers searched through the untidy, crowded rooms but it was Randan who had the first success.

"Sergeant, come and look at this!"

When Nathan entered the other room, he saw Randan was holding up a brown leather medical bag. When he opened it up, they could see it contained eight medicine bottles holding various powders and liquids.

"What will you wager that at least one of these bottles contains strychnine, Sergeant?"

Nathan smiled. "Now that's what I call prima facie evidence, sir."

"Indeed it is, Sergeant. I have also found this." Randan was holding up a wooden and metal board with grooves on it.

"What on earth is that, sir?"

"I'm not completely sure," replied Randan, "but I think it may be a pill maker, something that a doctor or pharmacist may use for making their own pills or capsules from the basic chemicals."

"That might be handy for anyone wanting to turn

strychnine powder into tablets, sir," suggested Parry.

"Exactly what I was thinking, Sergeant; let's keep looking."

Next it was Nathan's turn to stop the search. "Look at this, sir. I found it under the bed. He was pointing at a large and heavy typewriter.

Randan exclaimed, "I suspect that is what he used to type his extortion notes. Good work, Nathan!"

"It's one thing to suspect it, but how are we going to prove it, sir?"

"I fear you have not been keeping up to date and reading the latest works on criminal forensics. I trust that you are familiar with the work being carried out on fingerprints?"

"Yes, of course I know the theory that no two fingerprints are identical, though I'm not quite sure if I really believe it or not, if I'm honest."

"Believe it Sergeant! Before long fingerprints will be routinely used to catch, identify and convict criminals all over the world."

If you say so, sir," replied Parry. "But what has that got to do with typewriters?"

"Well, Sergeant there is other work being conducted by experts who believe that although characters typed on a typewriter such as this machine here may appear identical to the same words or numbers typed on a different machine, when those two pieces of typing are examined forensically, it becomes clear that the examples are actually quite distinctively different. In other words, if those extortion letters were all typed on this machine, then an expert will be able to establish that very fact. This typewriter, Nathan, is, I hope, yet another prima facie nail in our suspect's coffin. Have a look around and see if you can find any note or typing paper, flimsy sheets or carbon paper, anything related to this typewriter may also be important."

"I can't believe that he would be stupid enough to leave incriminating copies of his own letters lying around."

"Who knows? Just collect anything you find and we can have them forensically examined in due course."

After an hours searching, they had set aside the medical bag, pill maker, typewriter and a drawer full of paper, sheets of flimsy paper and used carbon papers.

"Have we looked at those books on the shelf by the window, Nathan?"

"Not yet, I was going to leave them until last."

"I think we have just about finished. Let's just check them before we go."

The books were all medical textbooks and a few novels but, just under the shelf, Nathan noticed a small notebook containing handwritten pages that looked like a homemade diary. "Perhaps we should add this to the pile of evidence, sir. It's just too dark to read it in this light."

"Let's take all this evidence downstairs and we can summon a hansom cab to take it back to the Yard."

It was past two in the morning by the time they had carried all the evidence up to the Criminal Record Office

"Let's lock it away in this store cupboard for now. It will be safe there until morning," said Randan and they both left the office to try and catch a few hours sleep.

When Randan returned to the office next morning at eight thirty he found Nathan already looking through the evidence.

"Do you want the good news or the bad news, sir?"

"Bad news first, I think. What is it?"

"You are summoned to see the Commissioner as soon as you arrive."

"Really? Well a cup of tea first, I think. While I'm making that, what's the good news?"

"I've had a look at this little notebook, sir. I think it could be really important. I think this idiot actually kept a diary and he has mentioned meetings with both Donworth and Clover!"

"Really? Could our day get any better?"

"Perhaps you should go and see what Sir Edward wants first before we begin to celebrate."

Perhaps *we* should go and see Sir Edward, Sergeant. Have you ever met him before?"

"No, sir."

"Then now is the ideal time to correct that."

The two detectives swiftly drank their tea and headed up to the Commissioner's office, knocked and waited to be admitted.

They entered the main office where Sir Edward sat stern-faced behind his desk. He looked questioningly at the young sergeant.

"This is Sergeant Parry, sir. He has been running the CRO since my secondment to the murder inquiry and he has been of great use to me at very short notice."

"I see," said Sir Edward. "I understand that you have already arrested a suspect, Randan, in Lambeth I believe?"

Randan smiled and said, "That is correct, sir. And Sergeant Parry and I have already secured a search warrant and searched his home address and secured what I think may be evidence of vital importance to this case."

Sir Edward did not appear impressed at this news. "That's good Randan, but I have some bad news for you."

"Which is, sir?"

"Your prisoner, Randan. Thomas Cream, was it?"

"Yes, sir. Dr. Thomas Cream. News travels fast."

"This news has travelled *very* fast, Randan. Cream is no longer in custody. He apparently escaped during the night. I think you'd better get over there as soon as possible."

Robert Jeffries

CHAPTER TEN

While Randan and Parry were executing their search warrant and looking for incriminating evidence at Cream's lodgings, Doctor Thomas Neill Cream sat on his hard wooden bench in his dimly-lit cell. He remained sullen and silent as he processed his thoughts. How had these stupid police officers managed to apprehend him?

It didn't take him long to realise that the police had been led to him by Hazel Peters. She would have to be taken care of in due course and he would enjoy watching her suffer for her treachery. However, he knew that he now faced more pressing matters. He could not deal with her while he was locked up and if the police found his medical bag containing the poison that he had used to kill Ellen and Matilda they would almost certainly have enough evidence to hold him in custody and possibly even sufficient to charge him with their murders. He didn't believe they could find any incriminating evidence other than the poison, but he couldn't be certain. Therefore, he needed to escape from custody.

When the goaler had removed him to his cell, the senior officer had ordered him to ensure that he checked on Cream at least every thirty minutes. Cream had already established that his goaler was a creature of habit. He estimated that he had been in his cell for about two hours, and he could expect another visit very soon.

Almost immediately, he heard the telltale sound of the heavy door leading from the charge room into the cell passage being opened. Then he heard the footsteps of the goaler and the rattling of the keys that hung from his belt. Cream knew that it would take the goaler ten paces to reach his cell; seven, eight, nine, ten. He listened for the click as the gaoler undid the catch on his wicket gate which, when opened, allowed his captor to look into his cell. Cream stared contemptuously with hate-filled eyes as his goaler observed him for a few seconds before slamming the small viewing gate shut and returning towards the cell passage door.

Cream estimated that the time must be about midnight. He had formed a plan.

A few years previously, he had had the misfortune to trip and fall and as a result of that fall he had hit his head on a wall which had opened up a gash on the top of his skull. He was amazed at the time that one small gash could cause him to lose so much blood and within a few seconds his clothes had become drenched with it. His plan was simple. He would bang his head against the wall of his cell and try and re-open the old wound. When his goaler checked on him in thirty minutes time he would find Cream apparently unconscious on the floor and covered in blood. With luck, Cream thought, he might be able to engineer an opportunity to escape as a result.

Ten minutes before he expected the goaler to return for his next visit, Cream stood a couple of paces away from the wall. He readied himself, then stepped forward with his head lowered to butt the wall with the top of his head, but all he managed to do was bruise his head and give himself a headache. He realised that he needed to be even more determined. He steadied himself again then launched himself full force at the wall. The force of the collision stunned him and he fell to his knees as a result but he smiled when he felt the warm blood trickling down his face, then he decided to heighten the visual effect of his injuries and hurled himself three more times against the wall. Now he lay exhausted on the floor and drifted into a state of semi-consciousness.

Cream failed to hear the goaler as he walked toward his cell. The goaler opened the wicket gate and gasped when he saw Cream lying face down on the cell floor in a pool of his own blood. The goaler ran back towards the charge room and shouted "Sarge! Call the guv'nor, quick. That bloody Yank 'as tried to top 'imself"

The duty officer, station sergeant and goaler all ran back into the cell passage and towards Cream's cell. The goaler fumbled with the keys in his panic to open the cell door and the duty inspector bent down to examine Cream.

"He's still breathing, one of you contact the divisional surgeon and tell him to get here as soon as possible."

Within ten minutes the divisional surgeon arrived in the cell to examine the prisoner. By now, Cream had begun to recover his senses and became increasingly agitated as the doctor examined him. "Get away from me you murderous dogs," he shouted as he started to struggle violently. The police doctor backed away as Cream's blood spattered all over him,

"You will need to restrain him Inspector."

The duty officer ordered the goaler to fetch the restraint jacket and once secured, it prevented Cream from struggling further.

The police doctor examined Cream as best he could and then advised the duty inspector, "I think this man should be taken to the casualty department at St. Thomas' Hospital. They should look at him. He will certainly need a few stitches. He may also need to be seen by a psychiatrist."

A hand cart was found and Cream was conveyed, still in his restraint jacket, to St. Thomas' Hospital. The final instructions from the duty officer to the three accompanying constables were, "At least one of you stays with him at all times. Do you understand me?"

The nursing staff were shocked at the appearance of the blood covered prisoner still in his restraining jacket. The sister in charge asked, "What on earth has happened to this man?"

The senior most constable answered, "Self-inflicted injuries, ma'am."

The sister raised her eyebrows.

Within a few minutes the casualty doctor arrived to examine Cream. As he bent to examine the wounds Cream whispered to him, "These wounds are not self-inflicted, Doctor. Those thugs at the police station did this to me because I refused to confess to their accusations. I swear it's the truth. I think they want me dead, but I am innocent of all their accusations. I'm a doctor, like yourself. It's my duty to save life, not destroy it, but they refuse to believe me."

The doctor said, "I'm going to need some privacy to examine this man."

The senior constable replied. "We have orders to remain with him at all times Sir. He faces serious accusations."

"I'm afraid you don't give the orders here, officer. I do. We will examine this patient privately in this cubicle and you will remain outside."

The officers looked at each other and the senior constable said, "It's alright, he can't go anywhere while we are outside the cubicle. You two go and stand on the other side of the cubicle and I will remain here."

The doctor and a young nurse examined and attended to Cream's wounds. "These will need several stitches and I think he will have to remain here for observation. This man may well be suffering from concussion."

"One of us must stay with him at all times Sir. Those are our orders."

"Very well," replied the doctor, "but I hardly think that all three of you need to be here getting under our feet. The other two of you can return to your police work."

The senior officer decided to remain with the prisoner and the other two returned to Lambeth Police Station.

Once Cream's wounds had been cleaned and dressed, he was taken to a ward on the first floor where he would be kept under observation. The accompanying officer was never more than a step away from him. When they reached the ward, the attending doctor said that he intended to remove the restraint jacket as the patient was now quite calm and therefore no longer needed to be restrained.

"I'm not sure that is wise, Doctor. He was very violent when he was at the station."

"Well, perhaps he had good reason to be agitated, officer. I am not at all convinced that all his wounds are self-inflicted and I will say as much in my report." The doctor removed the restraining jacket, handed it to the officer and indicated a bed in the darkened ward to Cream. "You will remain here tonight, sir, where you will be quite safe. You will be re-examined in the morning and then we will decide if you are fit to be released."

Cream smiled at the doctor. "Thank you so much, Doctor, but before you go, is it possible for me to use the lavatory before I get undressed?"

"Yes, of course you can, follow me."

The officer stood up to go with them. "Where are you going, sir?" said the officer. "I must go with him, sir. Those are my orders, to keep him in sight at all times."

"Really officer. This really is becoming quite tiresome. We are on the first floor. The toilet only has one door in and out. He can't get out any other way. You can wait outside the door and afford this man some privacy."

"No, sir. I must keep him in view."

"Dear lord, officer. Very well. You wait outside the door and I will accompany the patient into the toilet."

The officer was not at all sure. Before Cream entered the toilet, he checked the room for himself. It contained a lavatory, and a wash basin. There was one small window which was closed.

"Very well, Doctor. If you insist, but I shall remain right outside."

The doctor followed Cream into the room and the officer heard the lock slip into position.

"Don't lock the door please, Doctor, leave it unlocked."

"Thank you for your advice, officer", replied the doctor sarcastically.

Two minutes passed before the officer called out, "Are you all right in there, Doctor? Doctor, are you all right? Answer me!" The officer launched himself at the locked door which gave way on his third attempt.

In the lavatory he saw the doctor lying face down on the floor with blood seeping from a head wound. Beside him lay a heavy long handled wooden scrubbing brush. The window was open and as he looked down onto the Albert Embankment, he could see a tall figure running towards Westminster Bridge and he could hear a loud and excited shrieking sound coming from the same direction.

"Oh, bollocks!" muttered the officer as he ran through the hospital. He shouted to the ward nurse to assist the doctor while he ran as fast as he could to the exit. By the time he reached the Albert Embankment there was nobody in sight. He ran back to Lambeth Police station to raise the alarm.

Cream had waited until the doctor had turned away from him before hitting him hard on the back of his head with the heavy scrubbing brush. He then opened the small window and found a drainpipe immediately outside it. With considerable difficulty and effort he managed to squeeze his frame through the opening and then shin down the pipe to the ground below. He then quickly made his way towards the Albert Embankment laughing loudly and with a feeling of elation at once again outwitting everyone else in order to effect his escape.

Cream now needed a plan. He knew that he must not allow himself to be recaptured. Not even the incapable oafs in the London police would allow him to escape so easily a second time. He needed to clean himself up as best he could, then obtain a change of clothes. He wondered if he might dare to go back to his rooms at 103 Lambeth Road but he decided against this. The police had his keys and belongings and would doubtless have searched his rooms. They may even still be there and he certainly did not want to risk bumping into them again. No! His aim must be to get far away from London as quickly as possible. Maybe even return to the United States. Ideally, he wanted to clear up the loose end that was Hazel Peters before he departed. But she would have to wait. Right now he must head East towards London's commercial docks.

Cream made his way through the dark, deserted streets of Lambeth and Southwark. Eventually he crossed over London Bridge and entered the City of London. He walked quickly past the Tower and then passed through the St. Katharine Docks. He considered his best chance of making a quick escape was to find passage on a ship about to leave the London Docks. He approached the docks along Wapping High Street. There he saw a man dressed in working class, labourer's clothes who was decidedly the worse for drink staggering along the alleyway of Wapping Old Stairs beside the Town of Ramsgate public house. He approached the man in a friendly manner.

"Hello, my friend, are you sure you are all right?"

"Yeah, I'm fine, ta. I've just 'ad a little too much to drink." With that the man staggered a few yards further along the alleyway towards the steps that led into the River Thames itself. A little over half way along the alleyway, the man paused and leant against the wall for support. At this point, Cream approached the man unseen from behind, took hold of his shoulders and slammed his head hard against the brick wall. The unfortunate man slumped unconscious towards the ground and as his victim slid down the wall towards the pavement, Cream placed him in a reclining position with his back against the wall. Having checked once again that the area was deserted, he removed the man's jacket and trousers. He then took off his own blood-stained jacket and trousers and tried on his new clothes. They were far from a perfect fit but they would have to do. After all, he was seeking to stop looking like the elegantly dressed Doctor Cream and instead look like an East End labourer.

Cream then grasped his senseless victim under his arms and dragged him towards the water's edge. The tide was almost full and he found no difficulty dragging his victim down a couple of stone steps before casting him into the river. The body of the labourer settled face down in the water. Then his apparently lifeless form drifted slowly down-river on the gently ebbing tide. Cream watched casually and showed no emotion as his victim drifted silently away from the stairs.

The body became snagged for a few seconds on a mooring buoy before finally drifting free and disappearing beneath a moored coal barge. Cream then threw his own discarded jacket and trousers into the river and walked back along Wapping Old Stairs towards the main road.

Cream picked up his victim's cloth cap from where it was lying on the pavement and pulled it onto his head before returning to the deserted Wapping High Street. Under the glare of a gas streetlamp, he examined what he had found in his victim's pockets. He now had correspondence in the name of John Davies and as well as the change of clothes he also had some money in his pockets. In fact, he had all he needed to get himself a passage on a ship out of London. He had considered travelling first to Liverpool where he could more easily get a berth on a ship bound for New York, but that might be exactly what the police would expect him to do. Therefore, he would outwit them yet again. Now he planned to get a berth on a ship bound for Europe, possibly Hamburg and from there take passage to the United States and safety.

A few hours later Randan and Parry were standing dejectedly in the Commissioner's office as Sir Edward informed them of Cream's escape during the early hours.

"Do we know how he escaped, sir?" asked Randan.

"I've not had a full report as yet, Randan, but I can tell you that the management at St. Thomas' are hopping mad and complaining of gross police incompetence which has resulted in one of their doctors being seriously assaulted by a prisoner who was clearly not properly supervised. I am also expecting the press to be baying for blood with headlines about yet more police ineptitude. This is going to be a real mess."

Randan sighed. "I will go over to Lambeth and find out what actually happened, sir, then we will have to decide what needs to be done next. But there is one thing that we need to do as a matter of urgency."

"What's that, Randan?" asked Sir Edward.

"Cream will have worked out that Hazel Peters must

have played a part in his arrest, so we must ensure that she is put in a place of safety. She remains a vital witness for when we finally catch him again and put him on trial."

"Yes, of course, but surely he will be thinking mainly about escape rather than revenge, won't he?"

"Who knows what is going on in his mind, sir. But I do strongly believe that we have not seen the last of Dr. Thomas Cream and at some stage he will return, if only to prove that he can."

Soon after dawn, while Cream was scouring the London Docks in Wapping looking for a steamer to take him to the Continent, Inspector Peter Randan was once again walking to Lambeth Police Station.

Randan felt nothing but disappointment as he walked into the duty inspector's office. The inspector he had dealt with the previous night spoke in apologetic tones as he explained the circumstances around Cream's escape.

"The officer in the hospital, was he a young pc?" queried Randan.

"He was the longest serving of the three of them, but, yes, he was still inexperienced. That doesn't excuse his naïveté, though."

"I know that, but don't be too hard on him. We can all make mistakes when we are young and I am sure he feels wretched about what happened. He will learn from the experience and be the better for it."

"You are being extraordinarily understanding about this, if I might say so."

Randan smiled ruefully. "It won't improve the situation in any way whatsoever if we try to blame this all on a scapegoat."

The other inspector returned the smile. "It's interesting to hear you say that, because the superintendent I mentioned to you yesterday wants to see you in his office as soon as possible and from the look on his face when I saw him, I suspect he is most definitely looking for a 'scapegoat'. Be very careful with him. He is highly ambitious and will always be looking to offload any blame on somebody else's shoulders. Maybe yours."

"Thanks for the warning, I will be wary."

A couple of minutes later and Randan was on the second floor knocking on the door marked 'Superintendent'.

"Come in."

Randan opened the door and entered. "Inspector Randan, sir. I understand that you wish to speak to me?"

"Bloody right I do, Randan, come in and shut the door. What the devil do you think you are playing at? There will be all hell to pay for last night's fiasco and I hold you entirely responsible for the whole debacle!"

Randan stood his ground and looked directly at the senior officer as he replied, "I feel that is rather unfair, sir, since I was not in the police station or anywhere near St. Thomas' Hospital when Cream made his escape. At that time Sergeant Parry and I were executing a search warrant at Cream's address."

"Precisely!" exclaimed the superintendent. "Last night you arrested that man Cream on the flimsiest of evidence and brought him here on mere suspicion. If you had given that cock and bull story to me instead of the duty officer, I would have marched him straight out of this police station and let him go. In my opinion, you have displayed a complete disregard for the laws of this country and now your cavalier attitude has got the press sniffing around here looking for yet more evidence of police incompetence!"

"With the greatest respect, sir. I did and do have a great deal more to back up my arrest of Cream than 'mere suspicion' and that is amply borne out by the evidence that we found at his address."

"Evidence? I suspect the judge will throw out any so-called evidence that you found last night as inadmissible because your initial arrest was completely unlawful!"

"Once again, sir, I must disagree with you and although I have the greatest respect for your rank, I have no intention of standing here and bandying words with you. If I have allowed my zeal and enthusiasm to catch a dangerous criminal before he murders even more victims get the better of my sense of duty under the law, then I will expect to be properly disciplined by the relevant authorities. However, I don't believe that I have exceeded my authority in law. Furthermore, neither does the Commissioner, to whom I am reporting directly on this matter. I strongly suggest that if you have any complaints at all about my handling of this case then you voice your concerns to Sir Edward directly. Now, I have work to do and I will bid you good day, sir."

Randan spun on his heels and left the office, behind him he could hear the superintendent yelling, "You are insubordinate and impertinent, sir, and you may be certain that I will indeed be contacting Sir Edward regarding your appalling behaviour in this case!"

Randan walked along the corridor and winked at the duty inspector, who smiled back.

Randan left the police station and walked swiftly across Westminster Bridge. For a moment he considered going in and warning Sir Edward that he would probably be contacted by a very annoyed superintendent but decided to leave that for later. The previous day he had sent messages to Joan and Valerie that he would try to meet them in the Savoy Grill to update them on the case. When he had sent the messages, things were certainly looking a lot more positive than they were now, however, they would have to be told sooner or later. He stepped into the Savoy Grill and was met as usual by the ever-smiling Joseph.

"Good morning, Inspector, Lady Valerie and your colleague are awaiting your arrival. sir."

"Hello, stranger," said Valerie "I thought you might have forgotten about us."

Randan was unsure if Valerie's rather cold words were a sign of her displeasure. "I most certainly had not forgotten about you, but I have been somewhat busy over the last day or so, both Sergeant Parry and myself."

As he spoke Valerie at last smiled and handed him the late editions of the morning papers. "So we have seen. Have you read this?"

The detective read the headline. "Incompetent Police allow 'Lambeth Poisoner' to escape!"

"It really didn't take them long to get that story out, did it?"

"Why don't you tell us the real story, Peter; but, before you do, does Sergeant Parry look as exhausted as you do?"

Randan managed another smile. "Yes, Valerie, I imagine he does. We have both had a difficult day."

"I thought so. Joan, would you be an absolute angel? Go and ask Sergeant Parry to join us. I think our two heroes can both do with a decent meal then they can fill us in with all the details."

Twenty minutes later, the policemen were both demolishing a hearty lunch, much to the amusement of Valerie and Joan who remarked, "Dear me, you two don't look as if you have eaten at all for the last two days."

Randan replied, "I'm not sure that either of us have, Joan."

After his meal, Randan related the full story of the last twenty four hours or so, beginning with the observation in Lambeth High Street and arrest of Cream, and ending with his altercation with the Lambeth superintendent.

At the end of his account Valerie asked, "So, Peter, what do you think Cream will do now?"

He considered the question for a few seconds. "I think he will run, possibly he will seek to return to America. I will put out wire messages to all the likely departure ports and there is always a chance that he might be picked up, but I think it is highly unlikely that we will be able to stop his flight. Having said that, we can't be sure, it is possible that he may try and tie up loose ends before he disappears and I have told Sir Edward that we need to get Hazel Peters to a safe location. Cream will have worked out already that she played a large part in his arrest."

Valerie interrupted. "Peter, you can leave Hazel to Rose and me, she trusts us and I have the perfect hideaway for her."

The inspector immediately nodded his agreement.

"And what then, Peter? Is that the end of it? Do we just leave it there?"

Randan could sense her anxiety. "Most certainly not, Valerie. Our suspect may have slipped away from us but there is still evidence to examine and then a case to build."

Valerie showed her relief in her smile. "That is good to hear, but when we have sifted through the evidence and made the case against Cream as strong and compelling as possible, how do we get him to the Old Bailey to stand his trial?"

"That is a very good question, Valerie, and the short answer is that I don't know. Earlier today I told Sir Edward that I don't think we have seen the last of Dr. Cream. I truly believe that he will return to London again, if only to display his superiority over the police. I honestly believe he will be back and when he does return, we must be ready to arrest him again and this time we must ensure he stands his trial at the Old Bailey."

"Tell me, Peter, what sort of evidence are you going to need to gain a conviction?"

Randan thought again. "First, we have the murders themselves. I am hoping that we can link the poisons that I am sure are contained in Cream's medical case that we found in his rooms. Then we have the typed extortion letters that were sent to the Southwark coroner, Mr. Smith and Dr. Broadbent. I know that forensic examinations have been made of typewriters and typed documents and just as it is believed that no two fingerprints are identical, so there are those who believe that each typewriter is subtly different from any other. Even typewriters of a similar make and model and made in the same factories will display, when subjected to a microscopic, forensic examination, small but definite differences. I will be looking to prove beyond reasonable doubt that all three letters were typed on Cream's machine."

Valerie looked doubtful. "I have never heard of such work, Peter. Are you sure this can be done?"

"Yes, I think so. This type of forensic analysis is still in its early stages, but I am convinced that when we put all the evidence together against Cream, then our case will be compelling enough to convince any English jury of his guilt. Then of course, we may yet find even more prima facie evidence against our doctor. In short, we have a long way to go and much work to do."

At last, Valerie smiled. "And don't forget, Peter, not only do we have the resources of the Metropolitan Police to draw on, but if you need it, I can bring in experts from all over the world to look at the evidence and give their own considered expert opinions."

"I will leave you to sort that out with Sir Edward if we ever need to take up your generous offer, Valerie, but for now Nathan and I are going to return to the office where we can begin to fully examine our evidence from last night."

While Randan and Parry studied their evidence, Dr. Thomas Neill Cream sat below deck in a German-registered steamer as it moved towards the Thames estuary in the North Sea. His next step onto dry land would be in the port of Hamburg and from there he should easily be able to gain passage on a vessel bound for New York.

Cream was feeling extremely pleased with himself. He had comprehensively outwitted the London police to regain his freedom and soon he would be completely safe back in the United States. There he would be able to rest and reflect on his future. Surely the last thing that the police in London would be expecting would be for him to return to their jurisdiction. And yet, that was most certainly one of his options.

There were loose ends that needed to be cleared up. In particular, he needed to deal with and silence the treacherous Hazel Peters who had so nearly spoiled his plans by leading the police to him. Also, he needed to rub salt into the wounds of the capital's police force. The last thing they would be expecting would be for him to return. But return he would, and having dealt with Hazel Peters he would strike again! He smiled when he imagined the allegations of ineptitude and incompetence that the nation's press would hurl at the

Metropolitan Police for allowing a murderer to escape from their custody and then to return once again to continue his work amongst London's army of prostitutes. But this time, there would be no mistakes or errors of judgement. The infamous Jack the Ripper had killed five women and then escaped capture. He, Dr. Thomas Neill Cream, would cause even more terror in the nation's capital city and would then completely disappear, just as the wonderful Jack had done. But that was all for the future.

Late that afternoon, Inspector Peter Randan left his office and walked to the Savoy Grill and found Lady Valerie Meux in her usual booth.

"I was hoping you would come in, Peter. I know it's getting late, but I think we need to go and visit Teddy and get his nod of approval for what happens next, don't you think?"

Randan nodded his agreement. "Sir Edward is certain to come under a great deal of pressure from the press regarding Cream's escape and we should be able to give him some idea of what we have planned for the future."

They both walked the short distance along the Victoria Embankment from the Savoy Grill to New Scotland Yard. They entered the building by the small back door and made their way to the Commissioner's office. Their knock on the door was answered by Sir Edward Bradford's secretary who ushered them towards his private office and announced their presence.

Sir Edward looked tired as he sat behind his desk. Valerie apologised for disturbing him once more when he was so busy, but he waved her words away with a forced smile. "Has Randan brought you up to date with what has happened, Valerie?"

"He didn't really need to, Teddy. It's all over the papers and the press are having an absolute field day."

"Yes, indeed, and on Monday I must hold a damned press conference to explain what will happen next. Now, Valerie, I really do think it's time to end your involvement with this case. You have done a wonderful job, but I don't want you getting mixed up in all the nastiness that will doubtless follow."

"Come now, Teddy, I'm a big girl now and well able to look after myself when it comes to the gentlemen of the press and besides, Peter and I both have things we need to discuss with you and these things could be very useful ammunition for you to use in your press conference."

"Very well, Valerie, I will listen to you both, but first, Randan, I must give you yet another firm reprimand. I have recently received a complaint about your 'Impertinent Insubordination' from that ass of a superintendent at Lambeth. You really should not be doing that sort of thing to a senior officer. So don't do it again. Do I make myself clear?"

"Absolutely clear, sir," returned Randan trying to hide his smirk.

"Good! Now, what are these things that you need to discuss with me?"

Randan spoke first. "From what I have seen and read, sir, it seems that the press will seize upon each and every opportunity to attack our police forces in general and the Metropolitan Police in particular whenever a chance presents itself. The impression of a weak, inefficient and incompetent force is exactly what it wants to feed to the public simply because that idea sells papers. The press will keep up the attack on the police as regards Cream's escape for as long as possible. I believe that we must try and seize the initiative and therefore the press conference you are holding on Monday may well be a good idea. This case is far from over and we must now use the time that Cream's escape has forced upon us to our advantage. I'm sure the first thing that the press will call for is the dismissal of the officer in whose custody he was at the time."

"You mean the Lambeth pc?"

"Exactly that. sir; with respect, sir, I think you should refute those calls and explain that the officer concerned was young and inexperienced and that it is not your intention to dismiss an officer for an honest mistake, simply because the press think that should be the appropriate reaction. Secondly, sir, you can tell these gentlemen that the Metropolitan Police are, even as you are addressing them, building a watertight forensic case against Doctor Cream on several levels so that when Cream is once again captured – and you should also tell them that you are convinced that he *will be* recaptured, it's simply a question of when and not if!"

The Commissioner listened intently. "That sounds very positive to me. Thank you, Randan. What forensic evidence are we looking at exactly?"

"We are dealing with an extortionist and a murderer, sir. All three letters demanding money were typed. Sergeant Parry and I found a typewriter in Cream's lodgings when we searched it. I believe that by the use of expert forensic analysis we can conclusively prove to any jury's satisfaction that all three letters were typed on that very machine."

Sir Edward looked unimpressed. "Typewriters! I *knew* that nothing good would ever come of them!"

"If they can help us to convict Cream, sir, then perhaps even you might soften your views on them. You might even go down in history as the man who revolutionised written communication in the police, sir!"

"I wouldn't wager on that, Randan, if I were you!"

"We also found Cream's medical bag at his lodgings, sir. It had several bottles inside and I am pretty sure that at least one of those bottles will contain strychnine. I will have the contents of that bag scientifically analysed in the hope that we can match his drugs with the contents found in the stomachs of Ellen Donworth and Matilda Clover."

"Can they be that exact?"

"To be honest, sir, I'm not sure. But the only way we can advance the use of forensic science is to try and solve crimes using ground-breaking methods. If we do not try, how can we ever know for sure?"

"Ground-breaking forensic technology, eh? That's another term I can use on Monday."

"If I may continue, sir, I think it is essential that Valerie, I mean Lady Meux, remains an integral part of this investigation. It was she who convinced us both to take this case on and I think it's vital that she continues. I would even say essential, sir. Firstly, Hazel Peters may still be in danger. Cream must have worked out that she was involved in his arrest and I am sure he will wish to punish her betrayal of him. Valerie is best placed to keep her safe."

Valerie spoke again. "If I may interject, Teddy? Rose and I have already taken care of this. We have found Hazel and removed her to a safe location well out of London. She can stay there as long as is needed or for as long as she wishes for that matter."

"Excellent; where is she, Valerie?"

Valerie smiled sweetly. "I don't wish to be rude, gentlemen, but the fewer people who know her whereabouts, the safer she remains. Suffice it to say that she is safe, happy and content and she will be ready to give evidence against Cream if and when she is needed to do so."

Sir Edward again looked concerned. "This really is highly irregular, Valerie."

"Yes, isn't it just, Teddy? Look at it this way. You are quite right that she needs to be protected from Cream, but what might happen if some members of our beloved press discovered where she was being protected by your officers. Might not they consider her a legitimate target for their attention in order to gain yet more information which they can use to further attack the police?"

Sir Edward paled a little "The devil they would! Very well, I agree with you Valerie. Hazel Peters remains safely in your care."

Valerie spoke again. "One other thing from me, Teddy. All of these ground-breaking forensics that Peter just mentioned. It all sounds *very* expensive. You have my personal promise that my purse is open to you should you need, perhaps, to bring in forensic experts from overseas? Please don't be afraid to ask. I got you into this investigation and I have no intention of letting you down. And before you ask, my beloved Henry, Lord Meux, completely supports all of our efforts."

Randan rejoined the conversation. "There is one other very important reason why I want Valerie and Rose to remain involved with the investigation, sir. As she said right from the beginning, they have access to people and potential witnesses that we in the police simply do not have. Women on the streets have no reason to trust the police, sir. However, they have very good reasons to trust Valerie and Rose." Randan turned to look directly at Valerie. "Valerie, I will need you and Rose to double and then re-double your efforts with regard to your work with other women working the streets in the Lambeth area. I believe there are women living in Lambeth who have seen Cream in and around the local area. Possibly they can even link him with Ellen and Matilda, possibly other women too. If such witnesses exist, I need to find them, their testimony could yet prove to be of immense importance. By the way, Sir Edward, I wouldn't mention that part of our investigation in your press conference on Monday. We certainly don't want the press trying to further muddy already murky waters."

Sir Edward nodded his agreement. "One thing, Randan, do you think Cream is still in this country?"

The detective frowned. "I'm not a betting man, sir, but if I were to make a wager, it would be that Cream will make escape from this country his main priority. All the usual port warnings were sent out immediately and I suppose it is still possible that he may yet be re-arrested. But I very much doubt it. We don't really know a lot about Dr. Thomas Neill Cream but what we do know is that he is highly intelligent, extremely resourceful and possibly clinically insane. He is an extremely dangerous man. I truly believe he will return and when he does return, we must be ready for him."

On Monday morning when Sir Edward Bradford entered the meeting room at New Scotland Yard, he found the room packed with journalists. The air in the room was one of almost boisterous joviality and the men present were clearly expecting to enjoy the event. As he took his seat, the Commissioner of Police for the Metropolis wondered if this was the sort of atmosphere that once used to pervade a bear baiting pit. The men present were certainly eyeing up the senior ranking police officer as their potential prey.

Sir Edward spoke first. "Good morning, gentlemen. This meeting has been called so that I can advise you of the recent events in Lambeth following the arrest of a suspect on suspicion of two counts of murder."

Before he could proceed any further, he was loudly interrupted by a journalist sitting a few rows back. "I think we all know what happened already, Commissioner, we are much more interested in you explaining to us how it is that the Metropolitan Police can be so inept and incompetent as to allow a dangerous criminal to escape from custody. Have the police learned nothing from their recent woeful handling of other high profile murder cases?" This interruption was met with a loud burst of laughter from the rest of the journalists.

Sir Edward was possibly the only person in the room who was not highly amused. "Gentlemen, this meeting has been requested by your own organisations but as it is being held here in New Scotland Yard, I will decide how this meeting will be conducted. I intend to tell you all exactly what happened that night."

Once again, the same man interjected, "You mean you will tell us the police version of what happened that night, don't you?" Once again, the remark was met with raucous laughter.

Sir Edward drew a breath and tried not to rise to the bait. He at least managed to keep his reply civil. "I will tell you the truth about what happened and you will then doubtless go away and print whatever it is you wish to print, regardless of what the real truth is. But, gentlemen, I only have so much time available, so I would appreciate it if you can keep your amusing interruptions to a minimum. When I have given my report, I will accept a few relevant questions from the floor."

Another journalist pointed at the first journalist and taunted, "I think Sir Edward must have read some of your articles before, Harry!" which drew more laughs from the group but a scowl from the original questioner.

Sir Edward felt more settled after this minor victory. "Gentlemen, if I may continue. Three nights ago, acting on information received, two Scotland Yard detectives arrested a Dr. Thomas Neill Cream on suspicion of the murder of two women in Lambeth. This man was taken to Lambeth Police Station for questioning but was completely uncooperative."

The mood in the room was now much quieter and the journalists were all busily writing in their notebooks as Sir Edward continued, "Because the suspect refused to answer any questions whatsoever, it was decided to detain him in police custody while a warrant was obtained to carry out a search of his lodgings. That search revealed various pieces of evidence that may relate to the murders and other possibly related offences. However, as you are all very well aware, while the detectives were carrying out their search, it was discovered that the prisoner had managed to injure himself, we think, by repeatedly banging his head against the cell walls. He was immediately removed from the cell and officers rendered what medical assistance they could until a qualified police surgeon could be summoned to assess the prisoner's injuries. When that assessment had been carried out, the doctor advised the duty officer at Lambeth that in his opinion the prisoner should be immediately taken to St. Thomas' Hospital for a fuller examination. That was arranged and the prisoner was taken to St Thomas' Hospital by three uniformed officers. During his medical examination, the prisoner it would seem communicated to the medical staff that he was himself a physician and that his injuries were not self-inflicted but were in fact the result of a sustained beating by the officers in Lambeth Police Station. It would appear that these comments elicited some considerable degree of sympathy from the staff who became concerned for the prisoner's future safety. During the continued medical examination, the officers were told that they could not be present during the examination and that they would have to wait outside the cubicle. Following that examination, it was decided by the medical staff that Cream's injuries were serious enough for him to remain in the hospital for a period of observation. At this point, it was suggested by the doctor treating Cream that it should only require one officer to remain with the prisoner, allowing the other two to return to their normal duties. During his period of observation, the prisoner voiced a need to visit the lavatory. The officer initially insisted that he must accompany the prisoner into the cubicle, but the hospital doctor stated that this would not be in the patient's best interest because the room was too small and that he himself would accompany the prisoner. It was during that time that the prisoner attacked the hospital doctor and made good his escape through a window."

The first journalist again got to his feet. "So, what you are trying to tell us then, Commissioner, is that this violent criminal did not escape due the incompetence of the police but that it was all the fault of the doctor that the police officer had just allowed to be beaten to within an inch of his life! Oh, dear me. That explains everything…How could we be so foolish to believe that the police were in any way inept. It was really the fault of the hospital staff themselves. I have never heard anything so preposterous in my life!"

Another journalist rose to his feet "Commissioner, are you able to confirm that the officer who was supposed to be guarding this prisoner has been dismissed from the force?"

Sir Edward replied, "The officer concerned is entitled to a disciplinary hearing the same as any other officer. It will be up to that discipline board to decide what if any punishment or reprimand is due in this instance. Fortunately, gentlemen, there are rules and regulations in place for matters of discipline and whether he is dismissed or punished in any way will be decided by a proper investigation and not by a baying mob whose passions have been inflamed by dubious reporting." This comment caused an uneasy stir in the room, but it did have the effect of quietening the general mood.

Another journalist rose to his feet. "Commissioner, can you explain what will happen next? Do you think this murderer is still walking the streets of London or do you believe he has fled and if he has left the country is that the end of the matter as far as you are concerned?"

Sir Edward rose again to his feet. "I am afraid we have no information regarding the current whereabouts of this man Cream, but it is, we think, very likely that he either has already or is in the process of fleeing the country. We have taken all possible precautions in an attempt to prevent this from happening but, as I have already indicated, he is an extremely cunning and resourceful man. As regards what happens next? We still have much work to do. The evidence that we already have in our possession must be fully studied and examined and we expect that by using the very latest types of forensic and scientific analysis, we will be able to build a convincing case against this man which will see him eventually convicted at the Old Bailey. I can assure all of you here that absolutely no effort or expense will be spared by the Metropolitan Police in bringing this man to justice. The first questioner asked if we had learnt anything from past unsuccessful murder investigations? Well, I can promise you this. The best lessons are often those that are the hardest learnt. We have learnt much from our past efforts and where mistakes have been made in the past, we have tried to ensure they don't recur in the future."

"It sounds as if you are confident of catching this Lambeth Poisoner, Sir Edward."

"Indeed I am, sir, whether we catch him still in this country or if we have to pursue him overseas. I personally retain the belief that he will be arrested again and this time he will stand his trial. I also believe that we will have more than sufficient evidence to convince a jury of his guilt."

The first questioner raised his voice again. "Well, Commissioner, let's all hope that when and if you do recapture this man again, this time you can maintain a firmer grip on his collar than you have hitherto managed." Again the remark was met with laughter."

Sir Edward chose that moment to try to end the meeting however one other journalist rose to his feet and spoke in a rather patronising tone. "This is all very well, Commissioner, and thank you for giving us your thoughts on how you might catch this criminal who has already completely humiliated your whole force, but I would like to raise one point that you have thus far failed to mention. Sir Edward, my understanding is that the person running this entire investigation is not even a police officer. That is actually the case, isn't it?"

Sir Edward maintained a straight face and replied "No sir. You are completely wrong. This is a police investigation and it will remain so."

"Really Sir Edward? You see I am in possession of proof that the person running this fiasco of an investigation is a well-known socialite with no experience of policing whatsoever. Will you still deny it?" The final words were delivered almost with a sneer.

"Yes, I absolutely deny your allegation. My detectives are carrying out this investigation and will absolutely continue to do so.".

The room was now hushed and wondering where these questions were heading.

"Shall we stop beating about the bush, Sir Edward? I have proof that Lady Valerie Meux, a lady well-known for her frivolous excesses is in fact the person running this entire investigation. That is true, isn't it?"

At last Sir Edward smiled. "I don't know where you have obtained your 'proof', sir, but I do sincerely hope that you did not pay your informant too much money, because your allegations are baseless and your money has been wasted. You refer to Lady Valerie Meux as a frivolous socialite? That is your opinion and I suppose you are entitled to hold it. However, I know Lady Meux as a tireless worker for the least fortunate of women in and around the Lambeth area. It was in the course of this work that she discovered that two unfortunates whom she had been attempting to assist into a better life had lost their lives in highly suspicious circumstances. Lady Meux approached the Metropolitan Police and voiced her concerns. My detectives have examined her allegations and found them to be absolutely true. Lady

Meux is not in charge of or leading this investigation; she is, however, a vital part of it and I am most grateful to her for the assistance she has already rendered and has most generously offered to maintain into the future.

The questioner continued. "Indeed, Sir Edward. And these 'unfortunate women' that you speak of? Another way of describing them would be to call them 'common prostitutes', would it not?"

Again the Commissioner countered in a calm and assured manner. "You may choose to use that term, sir. Personally, I don't believe that women who live in a world where they see no other financial option other than to sell their bodies in order to scrape an existence should be described as anything other than 'unfortunate'."

Following this exchange, the journalists all moved swiftly for the doors to write their articles for the evening editions. One particular headline would read "Extrovert aristocrat leads hunt for the Lambeth Poisoner". The writer went on to speculate whether Lady Valerie would use her carriage pulled by zebras to catch London's latest killer.

Robert Jeffries

Chapter Eleven

For the next couple of days, Randan spent time in the Criminal Records Office catching up with some of the work that had accumulated in his absence. Fortunately, Sergeant Parry had proved to be an able deputy and there was not as much work to catch up on as he had feared. This gave him ample time to start planning how he would gather the evidence he would need to put Cream before a judge and jury.

Outwardly he remained optimistic that shortly he would receive a message informing him that his quarry had been arrested and was awaiting his collection somewhere within the country, but with each passing day he was forced to admit to himself that the likelihood of that happening was becoming ever more remote.

His office door opened to reveal the elegantly dressed figure of Lady Valerie Meux. "Good morning, Peter. I haven't heard from you for a couple of days and so I decided to pop in to make sure that you are not moping around feeling sorry for yourself."

The detective rose to his feet and greeted her with a smile "No, Valerie, I will admit to being frustrated with the position that we find ourselves in but I am not feeling sorry for myself. Not yet, anyway."

"I'm glad to hear it, Peter. The real reason why I am here, apart from wanting a cup of Joan's tea and perhaps one of her most excellent scones or tea cakes is to is to let you know that Rose and I are pressing ahead and making good progress with those inquiries that you wanted us to make amongst the working girls in the Lambeth area. I have already found one girl who also knows Cream and who can testify that she saw Cream and Matilda Clover in each other's company."

Randan raised an eyebrow. "Well done indeed, Valerie. That is exactly the sort of evidence that I will need to build up the greater picture that will have to be put before a jury. Please keep on along those lines and make a note of all the women you think might be able to complete that picture. I will then interview them with either you or Rose present and take their statements."

"How are your inquiries going, Peter?"

"At the moment, I am trying to work out a plan of action. I need to concentrate initially on the murder aspect of the inquiry, murder being the most serious of all the offences that we are investigating. I have already made an appointment for tomorrow to take a statement from the pathologist who carried out the autopsies and fortunately he can speak with great authority on the criminal use of toxins. His evidence in that area will be of great importance. I will also ask him to arrange for an analysis to be made of the chemicals in Cream's medicine bag. He should be able to confirm if any of the bottles do contain strychnine powder, as we suspect. I will also ask him to examine the pill-making apparatus that we found with the bag to see if it shows any trace of the poison on it. Unfortunately, with regards to the extortion side of the inquiry, I'm afraid I have hit a bit of a dead end at the moment."

"How so?"

At that moment Joan entered with a tray of teas and cupcakes.

"Oh, Joan, you are an angel and a mind reader. This is exactly what I wanted."

"This really is the very least I could do for you after all of the food you have provided for us at the Savoy Grill."

"Nonsense, Joan. And I have every intention of taking some of your cakes to let Joseph taste them. He might even want to place orders with you!"

Joan was beaming with pride at the compliments. "Thank you, Valerie, but I'm sure my baking must be very ordinary compared to what those professional chefs can make."

"Please sit down and join us, Joan. You may well be able to make some suggestions. Now, Peter, what were you saying about having a problem with the extortion side of the investigation?"

Randan steepled his fingers in his usual way as he framed his answer. "You remember I said that I believed Cream typed all three letters on his own typewriter and how I have read research that would indicate that characters typed on one machine can be forensically distinguished from the same characters typed on a different machine. In other words, no two machines will produce exactly identical results?"

"Yes, I think so, go on."

"Well, most of that research has been done in the United States and I don't believe Sir Edward will be overly keen for me to go across the Atlantic to prove my theories."

Valerie grinned at the detective. "Oh, really? If that is your major problem, then I may have a bit of good news for you! I have a very dear friend who is a professor and an expert on all things relating to the ancient Egyptians. He really is a most fascinating chap."

A look of utter confusion formed on the detective's face. "Firstly, Valerie, I had no idea that you were interested in the ancient Egyptians and secondly, how does that assist me with my inquiries?"

"Have patience, Peter. I have been fascinated by ancient civilisations and particularly with the Egyptians for quite some time now. In fact, I have a rather fine collection of my own at Theobalds Park and I am in frequent communication with Gustaf, that is the name of a professor who works at Heidelberg University. In my letters I have mentioned the matter of our investigations and also that we believe our suspect may have used a typewriter to compile his extortion letters. He replied to me saying exactly what you said. That a forensic examination of the typed letters and of the machine used by our suspect by a suitably skilled examiner could conclusively prove whether Cream's machine was used to type the letters."

"Forgive me, Valerie, but this we already know."

Valerie knew exactly how to annoy Randan. "Joan. These cupcakes are even better than the first batch you gave me."

"Valerie, can we please forget the cupcakes. What about your professor in Heidelberg? What else did he say?"

"Who, Gustaf?"

"Yes, Valerie, your friend, Professor Gustaf."

Valerie paused for suitable effect "Oh, nothing much really. Only that he has a very good friend who is also a professor at Heidelberg University who is something of an authority in this very field and only this morning I received this letter from Gustav. Would you like me to read it to you, Peter?"

"Yes, of course I would, Valerie."

Valerie removed the letter from its envelope and unfolded it. "It says, 'Dear Valerie de da de da de da, don't need all that … ah, here we are! I have now spoken to my esteemed colleague, Professor Schmitt and established that he is most interested in your investigation. If the police are willing to cover his expenses he will be very happy to come to London and examine your evidence relating to the typewriter and the extortion letters. If his examination proves that you are correct and the letters were typed on your suspect's typewriter then he will make a statement to that effect and attend any future court case if required to do so.' There, Peter, does that put a smile back on your face?"

"It certainly will do if we can persuade Sir Edward to agree to paying for his expenses. You know he is not particularly keen on typewriters."

"And that is precisely why I immediately replied in the affirmative. I will pay for Gustav and Professor Schmitt's travel expenses and they will stay with me at Theobalds Park while they are here. There is absolutely no need whatsoever to bother dear Teddy. Professor Schmitt can assist you with your evidence and I can entertain Gustav with my new ancient Egyptian acquisitions."

Now they all had smiles on their faces. "Do we know when they might be able to get here?" asked Randan.

"They will forward all the details by telegraph wire as soon as the arrangements are made, but I have already conveyed to Gustav that time is not our friend. So not long, I think."

Randan again steepled his fingers. Valerie, Lady Meux – you are a marvel."

Now it was Valerie's turn to blush at the compliment. "Oh, by the way. There is something else I need to tell you. Not such pleasant news, though, I'm afraid."

A frown wiped the smile from Randan's face. "What is it?"

"I fear we will have to cease using the Savoy Grill as our headquarters. At least for the time being."

"All right; is there any particular reason?"

"Yes, there is. Joseph sent a message to me today. It seems that since Teddy's press conference the other day, some gentlemen from the press have been hanging around outside the hotel. Apparently, they are keen to keep track of my comings and goings and I really don't want to be responsible for sensationalising this investigation any more than it has been already. Joseph tells me that some of the fools have even tried to offer him bribes if he will tell them when I am there and if I am meeting with the detectives in the case. How can they be so stupid? Everybody knows that Joseph is utterly reliable and incorruptible. Also, I am very fond of the place, and I don't want to bring it any bad publicity." Valerie's face showed a slight smile. "I am aware that this news will not annoy you too greatly, Peter. I know you doubted my idea from the outset. However, Joan, Rose and I had some very comfortable meetings there, didn't we, Joan?"

"Yes, we certainly did, it's a shame they have spoiled it."

"The good news is that Joseph will always treat you as my guests, if you ever want to use its facilities. But I don't think it can be our headquarters anymore."

Randan returned her smile and said, "It's back to slumming it at the Lyons Corner House for our special treats then, Joan."

"I suppose so," sighed Joan. " Every good thing must eventually end."

The next morning, Randan arrived at the office bright and early and found Nathan and Joan already at their desks.

Sergeant Parry looked up from his work "Good morning, sir. I wasn't expecting you yet. I thought you said that you were going to take another statement from the pathologist today."

"I'm going there directly from here, Sergeant. I need to take his first statement with me so that I don't repeat anything. I will also take Cream's medicine bag and that pill-making board that we found in his lodgings. The pathologist should be able to confirm if any of the bottles contain strychnine and also if any traces of the poison can be found on the board."

"I think that you having to come here first may prove most fortuitous, sir."

"Why so, Nathan?"

"Because I have just put a file on your office desk, sir. It came across the wire from the United States last night. I am positive that you will want to read it as soon as possible."

"Have you read it yourself?"

"Just enough to know that it's important, sir, and I am sure that you will want to be the first person to fully assess it. It's from New York and they are responding to the messages you sent out after Cream's escape."

Randan went into his office and examined the file. He quickly scanned the contents and discovered that the sender believed that his suspect was almost certainly identical with a man who has already been connected to several serious offences on the North American continent. There was even a grainy photographic image attached which was certainly very similar to Cream. He checked his watch and decided that he really did not have time to fully digest all this information.

Randan emerged from his office and handed the file to Nathan. "This looks very promising, Sergeant, but I mustn't keep the pathologist waiting. You have my full permission to examine this file and I will look forward to hearing your appraisal of its contents when I return. I really should not be overly long."

"Of course, sir. I will see to it immediately."

Randan collected the medicine bag, the pill-making apparatus and the statement and hurried off towards Southwark. In the meantime, Nathan Parry gladly put aside his usual boring work and settled down to examine this much more interesting file of information recently arrived from across the Atlantic. As he read through the file he jotted down with pencil and paper the salient points.

From the file, it seemed that Cream was born in Scotland but his family moved to Canada where he grew up and took up a career in the medical profession gaining a degree in anaesthetics, during which he had studied for a while at St Thomas' Hospital in London. It appeared that his misdeeds began quite early in his career. In 1879 he was suspected of performing several illegal abortions in Ontario and being responsible for the death of a woman named Gardener. However, there was never any prosecution or even any real investigation, despite the fact that there was good evidence that pointed towards Cream's involvement. There was also a suggestion that Cream may have also written a letter purporting to be from Gardener, blaming her death on a local businessman and attempting to blackmail the man concerned.

In 1880, he came to notice in the city of Chicago, Illinois where it was alleged that he was involved in the deaths of two women named Faulkner and Stack on whom he had performed illegal abortions. In the case of Stack, the report also mentions that it was believed that Cream may well have been responsible for a blackmail letter sent to the local pharmacist who had written her prescription. Again, no charges were brought.

In 1881, whilst still living and working in Chicago, he was believed to be involved in the death of a woman called Montgomery who, once again had died after an illegal abortion. On this occasion, the coroner ruled that her death should be treated as murder but there was hardly any investigation and again no action was taken against Cream.

It then appears that Cream's luck finally ran out later in 1881 when he was convicted of the murder of a man named Daniel Stott. It would seem that Cream had a relationship with Stott's wife, Julia and the pair of them decided to do away with the unfortunate husband. During the investigation it was suggested that Julia had supplied and administered the poison (strychnine) but it then seems that, perhaps when she realised she was likely to be taking the entire blame for the murder, that she turned state's evidence and all of the blame fell upon Cream who was sentenced to life imprisonment.

The story comes to life again after ten years have elapsed in 1891. Cream was released from prison when a plea for clemency was allowed. The file also suggested that a substantial bribe had been paid to someone in authority. The writer of the file suggested that this was the point when Cream decided to leave North America and head for London via Liverpool.

Some four hours later, Randan returned from his appointment with the pathologist.

"Did you get what you wanted, sir?" asked Parry.

"Yes, thank you, Sergeant, I already had most of the evidence that I required, but there were a few things that I wanted the doctor to clarify, particularly with regards to how much strychnine he had found in the bodies."

"How much strychnine does it take to kill someone?"

Randan smiled. "I asked that exact same question and the answer is that a poisoner who knows what he is doing will use about one gram of the poison, although the pathologist told me that in some cases as little as half a gram has resulted in death. It seems that Ellen Donworth and Matilda Clover had both ingested about one gram each."

"Was he able to assist with the medicine bag and the pill-making apparatus, at all?"

"Yes, indeed he was. He performed a test on a sample of the contents from the bottle that contained the white powder and he was able to confirm that it did indeed contain strychnine. Therefore, we can now assert that Cream had ready access to the same poison that killed both of our victims. Unfortunately, he could not say for sure that the strychnine in the medicine bag was definitely the poison that killed Nellie and Matilda. Neither could he find any trace of the poison on the pill-making apparatus as it had been thoroughly cleaned. However, I believe we have more than sufficient evidence against him without that. Now, have you made any progress with this morning's file, Nathaniel?"

"I have, sir. I'm sure you will want to go through it yourself but would you like me to give you a short précis and some of my thoughts on the matter?"

"A capital idea. But let's have a cup of tea first, shall we?"

Joan shouted back from where she had heard every word of their conversation.

"Cups of tea and scones coming up, gentlemen."

A couple of minutes later, the refreshments arrived in Randan's office "I think you should join us, Joan, I'm sure you will want to hear what is in the file."

"If you think that's all right, sir."

"Of course I do, Joan, you are an integral part of this investigation and besides I would like you to inform Lady Meux of what has happened. I am sure she will want to be kept up to date. Begin when you are ready, Sergeant."

Nathan Parry read through his copious notes while Randan sat listening intently with his fingers steepled in his customary manner.

When he reached the part where it seemed that Cream left North America and headed for London via Liverpool, Parry stopped talking and closed his notebook. For a couple of seconds, the room was silent.

Randan spoke first. "Thank you for that excellent summary, Sergeant, Can I ask you now to try and read between the lines?"

Parry looked puzzled.

"Yes, between the lines, Nathan. I would like to hear your thoughts perhaps about what wasn't mentioned. The report itself for instance. It did not strike me as an 'Official' report. To me it seemed like a series of observations by an interested third party, don't you think?"

"Now you mention it, sir, yes, I would agree with you about that, almost as if someone in New York had read your original warning alert and then decided to pull this information together and send it to us. There was a name attached to the report. It seems to have been sent by a Patrick O'Malley but there was no rank or title mentioned, which I find a little unusual."

"Does anything else come to your mind?"

"Yes, a couple of things, sir. The report mentions that although he qualified in North America, Cream did study at St Thomas' Hospital. That means that he would have had an idea of the layout of the place. You remember we were puzzled by how he seemed to know how he might be able to escape out of that toilet window? Perhaps he had been there before?"

"Excellent point, what else?"

"Well, sir, his whole modus operandi seems to suggest that he gravitates towards the 'red light' areas of large cities where he knows he can easily find his victims."

"Yes, I think you are correct. Possibly because he has learned that police officers pretty much everywhere seem to not unduly concern themselves over the death of prostitutes. Anything else?"

"Yes, one other important link between his supposed medical practices in North America and his murders in London. In the cases in Ontario and Chicago, it seems that he may have sent communications attempting to either attach the blame for his actions to other people or to try and extort money from innocent people whom he is attempting to blame for the deaths that he seems to be causing. It's a common factor and not one that I have come across in any other criminal case.

Again Randan smiled. "Exactly Nathan. I have never heard of anything even remotely similar before and I think it could be that one common factor that will eventually see Dr Cream meet his end at the end of a rope."

Robert Jeffries

Chapter Twelve

The following morning at ten, Lady Valerie Meux entered the Criminal Record Office at New Scotland Yard with a big smile on her face. "Well done, Peter, and you too, Nathan! Joan told me all about that report you were sent from New York, and it sounds like a huge breakthrough."

"Good morning, Valerie." replied Randan. "The report has certainly shone some unexpected but welcome light on our suspect, although it has also given us another mystery."

"How's that?"

Randan handed her the file that was lying on his desk. "This is the report that arrived yesterday from New York. It is certainly comprehensive and tells us a lot about Cream that we did not know before. Also, we have confirmed that the report is genuine in that it definitely originated from within the New York Police Department. However, the report is not in itself an official document. I have made an enquiry as to who sent the information but the department that would normally deal with requests such as mine says that it was not sent by one of their operatives. Indeed, their 'official' reports would not be nearly as extensive and informative as those sent to us by Mr O'Malley. That means that the person who signed the report perhaps intercepted my original message and sent this report in an unofficial capacity."

"But the information is genuine?"

"Yes, Valerie, I believe it is genuine."

The smile returned to Valerie's face "In that case Inspector Randan, the phrase that springs to my mind is 'Don't look a gift horse in the mouth!'"

The detective returned her smile. "You're right, of course. I just don't like mysteries."

"Now, Peter, how close are you to completing your investigation?"

"As long as Cream remains at large, my investigation cannot be completed, Valerie."

"Let me phrase the question differently, then. How much more work do you need to do before you are satisfied that your case for Cream's prosecution is complete?"

"I believe I will have reached that stage when your professor from Heidelberg University has completed his analysis and proven that the extortion letters were indeed typed on Cream's typewriter. There may be a few extra statements to obtain if you can find any more women who can give evidence about Cream's activities in Lambeth, but I think everything else is done."

"Excellent; in that case I have some good news for you. I received this letter from my friend Gustav in Germany, and he has confirmed that both he and Professor Schmitt will be arriving in London at Victoria Station next Friday week. I have invited them both to be my guests at Theobalds Park for the duration of their stay. I suggest that you meet them at the station when they arrive and escort them both to Theobalds Grove Station via Liverpool Street. We can check exact times, but I will meet all three of you at Theobalds Grove Station and convey you all to the house."

"I can then catch the next train back to London."

"Nonsense, Peter. I want you to stay for the weekend. Firstly, you should be there when Professor Schmitt is carrying out his analysis. He may well have questions he wishes to ask you about the letters. Also, of course, I know you will have questions to ask of him. Then, while you two are carrying out your analysis, Gustav and I can indulge ourselves in all things relating to ancient Egypt. I so want to show off to him how my study of hieroglyphics is progressing and besides, Peter, it will really be the ideal time for me to show you how much I appreciate everything you have done for Rose and myself during this investigation. It will be the best food you have ever tasted. I promise."

"What, even better than one of Joseph's breakfast grills at the Savoy?"

"Yes, Peter. Even better than that."

"In that case, Valerie. I will gratefully accept your kind and generous offer."

"Wonderful, that's settled, then. We can finalise times when I know when Gustav and his friend are arriving at Victoria Station."

Only a few days had passed before Valerie returned to New Scotland Yard and confirmed with Randan that the two professors from Heidelberg would be arriving on the boat train from Dover the following Friday afternoon. "They should be arriving at Victoria Station at two, Peter and I am hoping that you will be able to meet them both at the station. I have already sent Gustav a description of you and advised him that you will meet them outside the London, Chatham and Dover Railway Company left luggage office."

"May I ask why you chose that particular location, Valerie?"

"Of course. It's well sign posted and easily located and there should not be crowds of people hanging around outside. People usually choose well known locations and as a result finding someone you don't actually know can be like trying to find a flower girl at Piccadilly Circus. You really are spoilt for choice. When Gustav and Professor Schmitt arrive, they should have no problem identifying you. By the way, make sure you are wearing that brown derby bowler hat that you usually wear. I told them you would be wearing that when you meet them."

"You seem to have it all planned," laughed Randan.

"One likes to at least appear efficient, Peter. Now, we also need to discuss the evidence that you will need to have transferred up to Theobalds Park. I am not an authority on typewriters, but I suspect that Cream's machine is fairly heavy and cumbersome, am I correct?""

"You are indeed."

"Very well. I suggest that you make the machine and all the other bits of evidence that you wish Professor Schmitt to examine available to be transported from wherever you have it stored here, up to Theobalds Park by Thursday at the latest. Where shall I instruct my men to make contact with you?"

Randan considered this question for a couple of seconds and replied, "Probably right here in my office is best. Sergeant Parry and I will remove the items from the property store and have them here ready to go on Thursday. Just give your men my name and tell them to ask for me in the Criminal Records Office.

"Excellent, I think we have it all arranged."

"One other thing, Valerie; how formally do I need to dress for the weekend?"

Valerie pretended to look offended. "Peter Randan, If I even suspect that you might have any formal attire hidden in your bag, I will order the gamekeeper to shoot you on the spot. This is a working weekend and there will be no formality whatsoever. Everything must be perfectly normal. Is that all right?"

"Absolutely. I hate formal affairs."

The following Friday afternoon at two found Inspector Peter Randan at London Victoria Railway Station standing outside the counter marked London, Chatham and Dover Railway Company left luggage office. He checked his pocket watch and a few minutes later he saw two middle-aged, moustachioed gentlemen in what he took to be German country clothing complete with Bavarian style hats approaching him at speed. The leading man spoke in very good but heavily accented English. "Good afternoon, sir, am I correct in assuming that you are Inspector Peter Randan of New Scotland Yard? I am Professor Gustav Hessell, Professor of Antiquities at Heidelberg University and this is my colleague Professor Helmut Schmitt who will be examining your evidence over this weekend. Lady Valerie has told me that you will be guiding us to her estate at Theobalds Park. Are we ready to go?"

Randan nodded his agreement and after the usual handshakes helped the professors with their luggage towards the underground station entrance.

Gustav had already warned his companion that the next part of their journey would involve them travelling underground on a steam train from Victoria to Liverpool Street and Randan realised that Professor Schmitt was not looking forward to this part of the journey. As they awaited their train on the underground platform Professor Schmitt studied the other waiting passengers. As the steam-belching engine emerged from the tunnel the Professor remarked that it reminded him exactly of a scene from Dante's Inferno that he had once seen in Vienna.

Randan assured him that there was really nothing to be concerned about. Londoners were very used to travelling across the capital in this fashion.

"Really?" he replied, "I can't imagine me ever getting used to travelling in this vision of Hell with anything but primal fear in my heart."

"You must forgive Helmut, Inspector. He once studied theatre and the dramatic arts. Now he thinks everything is a show put on for his entertainment. Calm yourself, Helmut; we will soon be back above ground once again!"

Within thirty minutes the men were struggling up towards Liverpool Street mainline station. Randan sat his two companions on a bench to check on which platform their train would be departing from. Upon his return, he said, "Our Great Eastern train will be departing in ten minutes from platform four, which is just over there, so we can board immediately."

He guided his guests through the ticket gates and showed the attendant their travel warrants. Valerie had insisted that she would make up the second class tickets to allow them access to first class coaches. This made Professor Schmitt much more relaxed.

The journey from Liverpool Street Station to Theobalds Grove took about fifty minutes and when they arrived Valerie had arranged for the station staff to convey all their luggage to the road at the front of the station.

The smartly attired station master addressed the three travellers. "Gentlemen, Lady Meux has asked me to make you comfortable here until she arrives personally to escort you to her home. Please follow me."

The travellers were led into a side room where they were served with tea and sandwiches. About twenty minutes later they heard the sound of approaching hooves trotting along the gravel. Professor Hessel wondered out loud what interesting things Lady Valerie had planned for their weekend.

Randan assured him that Lady Valerie considered this to be very much a working weekend and that he wasn't expecting anything unusual to happen.

Professor Schmitt stood up and looked out of the window. "Nothing unusual, did you just say, Inspector?"

"Absolutely, Professor."

"And tell me inspector, is it not 'unusual' in England for carriages to be pulled by a pair of zebras? Because that is exactly what is coming down the road towards us!"

Randan rose to his feet and saw a smart carriage which indeed was being pulled by a pair of zebras. At the reins was Lady Valerie Meux herself.

"Good afternoon gentlemen and welcome to Theobalds Park; would you like to come and meet Jacob and Joshua who will be taking us all back to the house?"

As she stepped forward to greet her guests, the reins were taken by a uniformed groom who rode on the back of the carriage.

"By the way," added Valerie, "this is my head groom and driver, Mary Gee. She keeps all my zebras in tip top condition."

"How many zebras do you have, Valerie?" asked

Randan as he stroked the neck of the closest zebra.

"Only four here at Theobalds Park. Jacob and Joshua here are brothers and need to be driven together. Mary normally drives them on public roads but here on the estate I am able to drive myself. When I use a light cart, I usually have Isabelle to take me around the grounds. She is very calm, sweet and very easy to handle. We have also recently acquired a young colt named Percy and eventually he will team up with Izzy, but Mary says he will need more training before he will be ready to work as a pair. Up in town I keep some more zebras in stables close to Hyde Park. Once again, Mary will always drive me on public roads. It does tend to create something of an impression."

"Indeed, Valerie. I imagine it does!" replied Randan.

The bags were loaded onto the rear of the carriage. "Are we ready, gentlemen? Gee up Jacob, come on Joshua, let's take our guests home and show them round the estate."

Valerie insisted that professional talk and formal examinations should wait for the following day. She wanted Friday evening to be spent as informally as possible with everyone getting to know each other and for them all to be on first name terms with each other.

Valerie hadn't been exaggerating when she had promised Peter the best food he had ever experienced and although he was certainly no connoisseur when it came to wine, he guessed that the wines being placed on the tables would be well beyond his annual salary. The detective did not let it all worry him excessively as he was quite intent on keeping a clear head for his work with Professor Schmitt the following day.

After dinner, Valerie guided all her guests into the withdrawing room and they were offered cigars and cognac. Randan accepted a small glass of cognac which he guessed from the label may well have once graced the cellars of the Emperor Napoleon himself. However, he declined the cigars and he was pleased to see that his fellow guests also politely declined to smoke. Cigars and the accompanying taste and smell were something that Randan had never enjoyed or appreciated.

Valerie was delighted that everyone was relaxed and that the evening was going so well; however, it seemed that the excellent food and drink had made Gustav curious.

"Tell me Peter, I have known Valerie for a number of years through her excellent knowledge and keen interest in antiquities and in particular her expertise in Egyptian art, history and culture but never has she mentioned to me until quite recently her close friendship with an inspector in the New Scotland Yard detective branch. May I ask how you two first became acquainted?"

Randan coughed a little in surprise and glanced across at their hostess who now had a beaming grin on her face.

"That is a very good question, Gustav, but since it was directed at Peter, I think I will allow him to tell the story himself."

Randan coughed again and was aware that his face was probably reddening slightly.

"We first met many years ago when I was a very young police constable and before Valerie became married to Lord Meux. It just happened that I was able to render her some very slight assistance in a problem that she had at that time. We then lost contact and I did not see Valerie again until she came to me at New Scotland Yard. By now of course her circumstances had changed completely and in fact, at first I did not even recognise her when she introduced herself to me. She informed me that now as Lady Meux she was working with vulnerable and underprivileged women in the Lambeth area and believed that two deaths within that community that had been officially recorded as 'unsuspicious' may well in fact have both been murders. That is how we have come to be once again acquainted with each other."

"That is all very interesting Peter, but I am still very curious as to why Valerie sought out a police officer whom she had not seen for many years. Surely there are many other detectives that she could have contacted. Why you?"

It was the policeman's turn to smile. "Another excellent question, Gustav, and it is one I have often asked myself.

'Why me?' So now I will pass your question to our hostess and perhaps she will tell us."

Valerie looked at both men. "Oh, really, you men. So many questions! Isn't the answer plain and obvious?"

Her guests all looked perplexed.

"Gentleman, look at yourselves! You are all experts in your own fields of endeavour and expertise. Now that I am Lady Meux I can seek out the very best experts to assist me with my problems or enquiries. That is the reason why you are all here tonight. But the fact is, I have always been an excellent judge of character. When Peter and I first met all those years ago he did more than 'render me a slight assistance' in fact he probably saved my life when I had placed myself in a somewhat precarious position. Therefore, when I once again needed the help of a brave and discreet police officer, who else should I turn to?"

Gustav laughed "I note your use of the word 'discreet', Valerie. Perhaps one day you might tell us the full story?"

Valerie winked at the Professor "Not a chance, Gustav; not a chance!"

Valerie and her two German guests roared with laughter, but Randan was rather pleased that the questions were now at an end.

After some more polite conversation the two professors showed signs of tiredness after their long journey and excellent dinner. "Valerie and Peter, thank you for a most entertaining and enjoyable evening and tomorrow will be another fascinating day for us all. I am looking forward to seeing the additions that Valerie has placed in her collections of antiquities and I know that Helmut is eager to evaluate the evidence you have collected in your murder investigation, Peter, so we will bid you both good night and look forward to seeing you both in the morning."

Valerie answered, "Of course, Gustav, you must both be tired. Sleep well and we will all meet up again for breakfast in the dining room at eight."

When they had departed, Valerie offered Peter a nightcap which he politely declined saying that he too wanted to be fresh and ready to assist Helmut with his examination of the evidence and with that they both retired.

Valerie and her guests all gathered for breakfast at eight. Peter couldn't resist the grilled kippers. Valerie commented that she was pleased to see him taking advantage of an early meal. "I'm sure you don't look after yourself properly, Peter. Who cooks for you when you are at home?"

"I am very fortunate that my landlady is also a very good cook, and she sees to it that I don't starve."

"I'm delighted to hear that, although a good landlady is hardly a substitute for a good wife. A fine looking man like you should be married by now, Peter, and I'm amazed that some sensible woman has not snapped you up by now."

Randan almost choked in surprise and Gustav roared with laughter. "You see Peter, this is what you get when you associate with this woman. Not only does she want to solve your murder case for you, she also wants to act as your matchmaker!"

Randan quickly recovered his composure. "Thank you for your concern, Valerie but I very much doubt if there is much chance of me getting married. Police officers don't make very good husbands I'm afraid. I suspect it's down to the number of hours they have to work and the diverse company they are forced to keep."

Helmut chipped in "He has a good point. Look at him today eating breakfast with a member of the aristocracy and a couple of academics. Who knows where he will be next week? Perhaps in a police cell interviewing a serial killer!"

Randan smiled at the comment. "That would certainly be high on my list of things to wish for Helmut. But I doubt if it will happen next week. I might have to wait a little longer for that particular pleasure to arrive."

After breakfast, the group split. Valerie led Gustav towards her latest historic acquisitions while Randan and Helmut made their way to the room where the evidence taken from Cream's lodgings had been carefully laid out.

Helmut took with him a folder containing several sheets

of paper. "These are some test documents that I prepared at my university, Peter. You remember I asked you to send me copies of the three extortion letters that were sent to the coroner, the doctor and the businessman? I copied some of the texts of all three letters using some of my own typewriters that I keep at the university. I will this morning type the same texts using Cream's machine. When we compare the different examples, it should be a simple to task to say that the typewriter that you found in Cream's lodgings was - or was not - the same machine that was used to create the extortion demands."

Randan enquired, "Can we confirm first of all that the three extortion letters were all typed on the same machine?"

"Yes, of course, that is very easy to do." The professor picked up all three letters from the table. "First of all, let us look at the actual paper used. If we hold it up to the daylight, what can you see apart from the typing?"

"They all have the same watermark, it reads 'Fairfield's Super Fine Quality'. I hadn't noticed that before."

"Precisely, all three letters were typed on the same brand of paper. Of course, many people will use this brand of paper. It is a popular and well-known brand so in itself, this proves nothing. So first I must examine the three letters individually to see if I can establish beyond all doubt whether there are enough similarities in the three examples whereby I can say for certain that all three letters were typed on the same machine."

"And can you?"

Helmut examined each letter in turn with a magnifying glass. "Ah, yes, this is most interesting." After a little over a minute the Professor looked at Randan with more than a ghost of a smile on his face. "Yes, I believe so. I think it is best highlighted if we examine the lower case 'p' which appears in all three examples. If we examine each letter 'p' with a magnifying glass, tell me what you see?"

Randan looked closely at each of the three extortion letters and concentrated on each individual lower case 'p' "What am I actually looking for, Helmut? "

"Concentrate on the actual appearance of the letter 'p' in every instance where it appears."

"Wait a minute. I can see that there is a very slight … it looks like an imperfection on each and every lower case 'p'! It's very slight and most people would simply ignore it but it is actually on every single 'p' on all of the letters."

The ghost of a smile now turned into a broad grin. "Exactly right, Peter. I am now certain that all three extortion letters were typed on the same machine. If you look at all of my own examples, none of the lower case 'p's have that small imperfection. It is peculiar to one particular machine."

"But is 'that' machine Cream's machine?"

"Well, let us find out, shall we? Pass me that book of notepaper that is on the table, please."

Randan passed over the book of notepaper and Helmut removed a sheet, inserted it into the carriage of Cream's typewriter and levelled it up. He then depressed the 'p' key a single time before examining the letter with his magnifying glass. Then he tapped the 'p' key several more times and once again examined the result. After a brief examination with his magnifying glass, he said, "I think you will want to see this, Peter."

Randan took the glass and looked closely at the piece of paper which bore exactly the same imperfection as was present on all three of the extortion letters. He then pressed the 'p' key a dozen more times himself in sheer pleasure. "But what causes that tiny imperfection, Helmut?"

"Well, each key is connected to a lever within the machine which strikes the inked ribbon and leaves the required character on the paper." Helmut pressed the 'p' key and raised it slightly; he then held the striking lever in his fingers and examined it with the magnifying glass. "There! Look, Peter, you can see that the imperfection is visible on the striking part of the lever itself. What caused it? Who knows? Probably a tiny speck of something in the manufacturing process. It's not enough for the whole thing to be rejected but *just* enough for us to prove the unique nature of this particular machine!"

It was Randan's turn to grin. "Lucky for us, then Helmut, but very unlucky for the good doctor! But is that it? Will that be enough to prove that Cream is guilty of sending the three extortion letters?"

"No, no, no, Peter, This is just the start of my work for today. I myself am fully convinced that the extortion letters were created on the same machine and that the machine that you found in Cream's lodgings is the very machine that created all three letters. Now I must fully examine everything you have here and find as many other examples of similarities like the lower case 'p'. Then I must compare the colour of the typewriter ribbon and see if it is consistent with the colour used on all three extortion letters. This all builds up the case against your suspect. The one slight imperfection on the letter 'p' will not be enough to convince a jury. But I will build a comprehensive and compelling case to put before the jury. I might not be able to prove that Cream is a murderer, that, my friend, is your job, but I do intend to prove to the jury that he is beyond doubt our extortionist. And I am hoping that somewhere on this table is the one bit of evidence that will seal his fate. I'm not actually sure what it might be. The man is not a fool so he wouldn't have used carbon papers, which is a shame."

"Carbon papers, Helmut? What do you mean?"

"Ah, I am sure you are aware that if you want to create a copy of what you are typing then you can do so by putting a sheet of carbon paper behind your original sheet of paper and behind that you place another sheet of ordinary paper so that when the lever makes an impression on the first sheet of paper, an exact copy is created on the second sheet of paper behind the sheet of carbon. But no criminal mastermind is going to create and retain copies of his own extortion letters that could be used against him in court."

"No, I take your point and I'm afraid that we didn't find any copies of his letters in his lodgings. But he did sometimes use carbon paper, and I think they all are all in that folder over there."

"Really? Let us have a look." In the folder were about a

dozen sheets of black carbon paper. Helmut looked at the sheets with his magnifying glass and swiftly discarded the first six sheets. The next two sheets he examined very closely. "Oh, my word, Peter, I think we may have just found that 'one' piece of evidence that I mentioned before. This could prove conclusive. Look at this first sheet of carbon paper. It has been used several times but look at the bottom part of the sheet and you can plainly see the exact words that were on two of the extortion letters and on this second sheet it is even clearer. This sheet has only been used a couple of times and I can make out pretty much the entire letter that was written to Dr. Broadbent. The fool really did make copies of his own extortion letters. He may have destroyed the actual copies, but these sheets of carbon paper confirm they were certainly typed on his machine!"

All day the two men worked hard on establishing as many separate 'similarities' that linked Cream's typewriter with the extortion letters and together with the sheets of carbon paper Helmut was now convinced that the link between Cream, his typewriter and the extortion letters was, in his own words 'incontrovertible'.

Randan and the professor had completed their work by early Saturday evening and both decided to have a rest before dinner. Randan retired to his room, kicked off his shoes and lay on his bed contemplating what he needed to do next. Professor Schmitt's completed report would draw a line under his investigation. He had taken the case as far as the available evidence would allow him. All the available evidence had been gathered and all the witness statements had been signed and filed. All he needed now was for Cream to be arrested so that the evidence could be placed before a judge and jury.

Dinner that evening was a very happy affair. Gustav had made some very flattering remarks about Valerie's collection of Egyptian antiquities and she was positively glowing with pride at his comments but most of the conversation centred on Helmut's findings. Valerie said, "I think you have done wonderfully well, Helmut. To conclusively link Cream with those extortion letters is an amazing achievement and will go a long way to proving his complete guilt."

"Thank you, Valerie. Let us all hope you are right."

"Peter, I think we must inform Teddy of Helmut's discovery as soon as possible. I really can't wait to see the look on his face when he hears that evidence provided by, of all things, a humble typewriter could help to prove Cream's complete guilt."

During dinner, the detective was noticeably quiet and withdrawn. Valerie asked him if he felt unwell.

"I am very well, thank you, Valerie, I just wish I knew when and indeed if we will ever get the chance to put our friend Doctor Cream on trial."

"That is a problem for another day, Peter. Tonight, your role is to help me keep our guests entertained and that glass of wine that you are toying with is not going to drink itself! Let us all enjoy our last night together and worry about Dr Cream some other time."

A smile returned to the detective's face and the four of them enjoyed a most excellent dinner.

After breakfast on Sunday morning the guests prepared themselves to leave Theobalds Park. Their luggage was loaded onto the zebra cart and Mary Gee took the reins of Jacob and Joshua to take them all to the station. At noon Valerie wished the professors 'bon voyage' as the train departed for Liverpool Street and at two thirty Randan waved farewell to them as they boarded their Dover bound train at Victoria, before heading home to his lodgings.

Robert Jeffries

Chapter Thirteen

Monday morning proved to be something of an anticlimax. Randan and Valerie had their interview with Commissioner Sir Edward Bradford and Valerie completely failed to hide her amusement when he turned up his nose at the very thought that the hated typewriters might actually play an important role in convicting the murderer.

After the interview, Randan returned to his desk at the Criminal Records Office and resumed his normal role. The only change was that Sergeant Nathaniel Parry had been confirmed in his role working alongside Randan and Joan and there was certainly enough work in the office to keep them all busy.

Days turned into weeks and weeks into months. At first Randan thought about the murders on a daily basis but as time passed the names of Ellen Donworth and Matilda Clover came to his mind less frequently.

For her part, Lady Valerie Meux returned to her work with vulnerable women in Lambeth with Rose. At first, she was often in touch with Randan at New Scotland Yard but again as the weeks passed her contacts and communications became less frequent.

On the occasions when Randan did think about the murders, he found himself becoming increasingly dispirited. At first, he considered that it would be only a matter of time before Cream would return to London but, as time passed, he began to wonder if his optimism had been misplaced. After all, Cream could justifiably claim that he had quite literally got away with murder! If he chose to remain in the United States, he would know very well that his chances of being arrested were very small. Why on earth would he take such a risk? He would have to be mad to return to London! Yet Randan clung to that slim hope.

At mid-morning on Thursday, April 14th 1892 Randan was sitting at his desk working through a large pile of criminal record files when Joan knocked and entered his office. "There is an American gentleman outside who would like to speak to you, Inspector Randan."

"Can Sergeant Parry deal with him, Joan? I'm up to my neck in these files at the moment."

"He's out of the office at the moment, sir, and I really do think that you will want to speak to this man yourself."

"Why so, Joan?" he replied, trying to hide his irritation.

"Because his name is Patrick O'Malley from the New York Police Department. Ring any bells?"

"O'Malley is here? Now? Why on earth didn't you say so, Joan! Show him in, oh, and a pot of tea and some of your very best scones too and when Sergeant Parry returns you had better both come in to hear what he says."

O'Malley was a tall and well-built young man probably, Randan estimated, in his mid-thirties. Randan stood as he entered his office and thrust out his hand in greeting. "Mr. O'Malley, welcome indeed to New Scotland Yard, may I ask to what we owe this most unexpected honour?"

O'Malley returned the detective's welcome with a firm handshake and a warm smile. His accent was very much that of a native of New York City. "I can assure you Inspector Randan that the honour is entirely mine. My main reason for being in London is to meet my extended London family but I was always minded to come along to New Scotland Yard when I had the opportunity. However, events have taken an unexpected turn during my visit and I now find myself, I suppose you could say, 'duty bound' to come and consult you.

I believe you will be most interested in what I have to tell you."

Before the visitor could continue Sergeant Parry and Joan entered the office bearing trays of refreshment.

"Excellent timing, Nathaniel. This is Patrick O'Malley from the New York Police Department, and it sounds as if he may have new information to give us."

Parry asked if he should fetch Lady Valerie. "No time for that I'm afraid. Perhaps, Joan, you could jot down some notes and we can relay all the facts to Valerie when the time comes. Please help yourself to Joan's most excellent cakes and tell us why you are here, Mr O'Malley."

The American took a swig of tea and a bite of the scone and began to talk. "As you can tell from my accent, I am an American, born and bred in New York City but both my parents travelled to America from London although, as you might guess from my name, they both originated in Ireland. Mum and Dad both left Ireland and headed to London looking for those famous 'golden pavements' but they both quickly realised their mistake and all they found in Lambeth, where they settled because they had some other family members also living in that area, was slum conditions and grinding poverty. Anyway, they did find each other and when Mum found herself expecting me, they both decided that they had to move on. They could not return to Ireland, so my father invested everything in a couple of one-way tickets to New York."

O' Malley took another sip of tea and nibbled a scone before continuing. "When they arrived, they found a thriving Irish community, Dad easily found work and they both settled down to their new lives as Irish Americans. They insisted that I should have a good education and I was pretty good with my schoolwork. Mum and Dad wanted me to undertake some sort of office or business work, but I had my heart set on a life of action. I thought about going to sea but a guy I knew persuaded me to join the NYPD and I worked as a patrolman in various divisions before applying for the Detective Department. I have performed various roles within the department and my current job involves me collating and evaluating information from the harbour area around Brooklyn. This is work that particularly suits me because it affords me ample time and opportunity to keep in touch with the London side of my extended family. I believe that police humour is pretty universal and when my colleagues found out about my Irish/English roots they nicknamed me Paddy Limey."

He sipped his tea again. "In my work I have to trawl through official and newspaper reports from all over the world and obviously I spend quite a bit of my time checking on the English news and press reports. That was when I picked up on the murders of Donworth and Clover and the subsequent arrest of Dr. Cream. As soon as I read that he may be heading back Stateside I began to gather whatever information I could and when your wire report arrived at the NYPD, I was the obvious man to deal with it."

"But why are you here, Patrick?" interjected Randan.

"In my job I have gathered a lot of contacts in businesses around the harbour area and when I re-read your reports, I noticed that you mentioned that Cream may well try and return to London so I circulated his photo and details around some of the shipping companies in the hope that it may draw a response. A few days later, I received notification that someone matching Cream's description, but using the name of John Davies, had left New York bound for Liverpool. I contacted my senior officer with the intention of informing you but my boss said, 'When was the last time you saw your family in London?' I told him that I had never seen any of them to which he said, 'By the time he gets to Liverpool and then down to London, you could be close on his heels. Take some leave, but remember you are not a cop in London, just a visitor.' So I pulled in some favours, got a cheap passage to London and made for Lambeth where I am staying with my extended family."

"Your senior officer is a very generous man to just let you go like that, Patrick."

"He is, Inspector, but he has always been someone who

looks at problems from a different angle. Plus he knew that I had quite a bit of leave outstanding which had to be taken."

"Have you managed to discover if the man heading for Liverpool really was Cream?"

"I'm coming to that, sir. One of the reasons why I didn't come directly to New Scotland Yard was because my information might be wrong and so I decided to do some private investigation mixed in with a little sightseeing with my cousins. They took me on a tour of Lambeth pubs that Cream might have visited to search for his victims. Two nights ago, that's Tuesday night, my cousins took me to Gatti's Music Hall in Westminster Bridge Road. They introduced me to a friend of theirs, they said her name was Susie Wilton but everyone seemed to know her as 'Susie Rags'. I asked her why? She laughed and told me it was because that was how she made her money, by collecting old rags and selling them to be pulped and re-used. This was all new and fascinating for me. I went to the bar to buy Susie and my cousins a drink when a man tapped me on the shoulder and said, 'You are a long way from home. By your accent I'd say you are a native New Yorker. Are you a sailor?' As I looked at him, I could hardly believe what I saw. He was so much like the photograph I had sent you from New York. I simply could not miss the squint in his eye. I realised immediately I was being addressed by Doctor Thomas Cream himself, although he told me that his name was Thomas Harrison. I had trouble containing my excitement, but I remembered what my boss had said about me having no power of arrest in London, so I decided that keeping close to the truth was my best route. I told him that I was a clerk in New York who was taking perhaps my only chance to come to London to visit my extended family. He told me that I was off the usual tourist routes and that Lambeth could be a dangerous place for unwary strangers. I pointed to my cousins and assured him that I was in good hands. However, I also added that I was very interested in criminality in London and I had wanted to visit some of the seedier places. It was then that I mentioned the murders of last year that had been attributed by the press to 'The Lambeth Poisoner' and that my cousins had said that this is a place where the killer might have looked for his victims. At this his eyes lit up. 'Oh, why didn't you say so straight away? I followed that case very closely and indeed I consider myself something of an authority on those killings. Would you like me to take you around the places where Doctor Cream would have visited during his time in London?' I agreed that this would be an ideal and exciting opportunity to learn more about these murders. At first, he wanted to charge me a pound for a tour. I pleaded poverty and we eventually agreed on a shortened version of the tour for ten shillings and I arranged to meet him outside the Mason's Arms Pub in Lambeth Road at noon yesterday."

O'Malley paused to sip his cooling tea and take another nibble of a scone. "When we met as planned, I was surprised to see him dressed exactly as you described him in your reports, complete with top hat and monocle. He told me that to truly understand the nature of the man one has to enter his personality. I asked him what sort of man he considered Cream to be, and he told me that in his opinion the reason why the police investigation had been so woefully inadequate was because they underrated his ability. He told me that he considered Cream to be one of the foremost criminal minds of this age. We walked around the area, and he showed me his address at 103 Lambeth Road. Then he showed me where he had first met Ellen Donworth and Matilda Clover. I suggested to him that now Cream is safely back in the USA the case must be closed. At this remark he just smiled and said, 'Really? what on earth makes you say that?' I asked him why Cream would risk returning to the city where he was wanted for murder and he answered me by saying, 'Because he knows he is safe. He escaped once and he can do it again! He will be in and out of London having completed his work before the imbecilic London police realise that he has even returned.' I said to him, 'You speak as if he is already in London,' to which he replied, 'He is back in London, I have seen him myself!' I feigned surprise and asked him where? He just said that he had seen his reflection in a shop window, but he was positive it was Cream. 'And I can tell you something else, young man. He has already started killing again. Already he has slaughtered three more women and the police have absolutely no idea who they are or how they died.' I told him this was too remarkable to believe, how could he be sure? All he said was, 'You can do what I did and check the information for yourself. Their names are Louise Harvey, Alice Marsh and Emma Shrivell. The last two he killed together only a few days ago."

Randan interrupted him with a sense of urgency in his voice. "Stop there, Patrick, you are telling us that he has returned and started killing all over again?"

"That's what he said, sir. That was yesterday. I immediately found out how to get to New Scotland Yard and came here last night hoping to see you, but I was too late. This was the earliest I could get here."

"Thank you, Patrick. You have already mentioned that you recognised his severe squint, did you notice anything unusual about his voice?"

"You mean did it raise almost to a squeak when excited? Yes, that too. Cream is back in London, Inspector Randan. I am quite sure of it."

Peter Randan sat quietly for a few seconds as the importance of what he'd just been told sank in. "We need to move swiftly. If Cream believes that we are as yet unaware of his return, that gives us an advantage. Patrick, you have done well and even though your position in the New York Police Department confers no lawful powers on this side of the Atlantic, as of now, you are an important part of this inquiry. Can I assume that you wish to be actively part of our investigation?"

The American detective smiled broadly back "You may indeed assume that, Inspector. I will do whatever I can to assist."

"Excellent; you and I are going to pay a visit to the Southwark Coroner's office to find out what he can tell us about Cream's latest victims. Sergeant Parry and Joan, will you please go and find Valerie and apprise her about what we have just heard from Patrick? I need to know if there is anything she can tell us about these three latest victims."

Thirty minutes later, Randan and O'Malley were entering the Southwark Coroner's office. Randan introduced the American detective. "Doctor Pullman, there has been a new and important development in the case in which Ellen Donworth and Matilda Clover were murdered last October. It appears that the man we strongly suspect of those murders has returned to London and I have reason to believe that he has already murdered another three women in Lambeth."

The coroner looked shocked. "What can I do for you, Inspector?"

"Detective O'Malley here has spoken to a man who, though he used another name, we believe, is in fact our suspect, Dr Thomas Cream. This man claimed to have detailed knowledge regarding the murders and of Dr. Cream himself. It was this man who revealed to Detective O'Malley that Cream is active once again in Lambeth and he gave him the names of three women whom he claims Cream has murdered since his return. Do the names Louise Harvey, Alice Marsh and Emma Shrivel mean anything to you?"

Dr. Pullman reached for his records. "The second two names are known to me, Inspector. The bodies of Alice Marsh and Emma Shrivel, both believed to be prostitutes, were discovered together in somewhat suspicious circumstances last Tuesday morning, April 12th. The cause of death was not initially obvious. I only received the autopsy report back yesterday and it confirmed they were both poisoned. I must admit that I thought of your cases as soon as I saw the report but because your killer had escaped back to America, I did not believe these two deaths could be connected with your investigations from last year."

"I see, what about the other woman, Louise Harvey?"

"That name is not known to me, Inspector."

"Please check your records again, sir. The man who was talking to Detective O'Malley was quite emphatic that Cream had also killed Harvey. Perhaps she could have come in under a different name?"

Pullman carefully rechecked his records. "No, she has definitely not come through this office, in fact we have no other cases of poisoning outstanding at all. I suppose she may have been dealt with by another coroner's office. I can check that for you, it shouldn't take long."

"I would be most obliged, Doctor, Thank you. One last question, sir. How were Marsh and Shrivel poisoned?"

"Each had ingested a gram of strychnine. They would both have died slow and agonising deaths. You need to catch this man, Inspector."

Both detectives left the Coroner's office and headed back towards New Scotland Yard. A short while after their return, Sergeant Parry and Joan arrived back with Valerie. Randan made the necessary introductions and Detective O'Malley smiled.

"I'm delighted to meet you, Lady Meux. I've read quite a lot about you in the English newspapers that I read in New York. They were fascinated by the aristocratic lady who was assisting the London detectives with their inquiries so it is indeed a real pleasure to meet you at long last."

Valerie returned his smile "You mustn't believe everything you read in the press, Detective; my role in this matter has really been quite small but I convinced Inspector Randan that I have some specific knowledge that might assist him in his investigations."

Randan interrupted her. "Specific knowledge that I need to test yet again, Valerie. Did Joan tell you the identities of the latest believed victims, Harvey, Marsh and Shrivell?"

"Yes, she did. And they present us with something of a dilemma. Marsh and Shrivell are unknown to me. They are not part of our project. But Louise Harvey is well known to us, but here is the problem. Joan and Nathan told me that she was killed on or around the 3rd of April?"

"Yes, that is our information."

"Well, if that is indeed the case, Peter, she has a very healthy ghost still walking around in Lambeth. I saw Louise only two or three days ago and she was very much alive."

"We need to speak to her as a matter of urgency, Valerie. Can you take us to her?"

"Yes, but we will have the similar problem that we had with getting close to Hazel. She will run far and fast if I take you directly to her, so I suggest we use the same method that worked with Hazel. We send Rose in to prepare the ground and assure Louise that she has nothing to fear from you."

"Agreed, but again, there is absolutely no time to lose."

That afternoon saw this strange group navigating their way through the ugly tenement housing blocks inhabited by Lambeth's poorest, destitute and desperate inhabitants. When they neared the block where Louise Harvey rented her rooms, Rose entered on her own. About ten minutes later she reemerged in the company of a thin, dark-haired woman who she introduced as Louise Harvey. They made their way to the small refreshment rooms where Valerie and Rose held their meetings.

Randan began, "Thank you for meeting us, Miss Harvey. I believe that you may be able to assist us with a very important matter which is connected to the deaths last year of Ellen Donworth and Matilda Clover, with whom, I believe, you were acquainted."

Louise nodded "Yeah, I knew 'em both very well an' it was tragic what 'appened to 'em but I don't sees as 'ow I can help. The papers all reckoned that their killer escaped 'cos the police were useless. No offence meant, but 'ats what they said."

"Yes, I know what the papers said, Louise. The fact is that we believe the murderer may have returned and is intent on killing again. This gentleman is a detective from New York City in America and he believes that he was actually speaking to the murderer only yesterday, although he used a different name. During their conversation he claimed Ellen and Matilda's murderer had already killed another three women since his return, and yours was one of the names he spoke of."

"Then he's a liar, ain't he? 'Cos here I sits talking to you and quite obviously I ain't dead."

Randan produced Patrick's photo of Cream from his

jacket pocket. "Would you look closely at this photo please Louise. Do you recognise this man?

Louise took one look at the image and laughed. "Him? Yeah of course I know him. I met him last week and he was a very strange bloke. I took a dislike to him as soon as I clapped eyes on him. When you work on the streets you develop what I calls my 'sixth sense'. This bloke was weird and he just gave me the creeps."

"Can you recall anything particularly strange about him or the things he said or did?"

"Yeah, he had a yank accent but sounded well educated. 'E told me he was a doctor."

"Anything unusual about his voice?"

"Yeah. It would be normal one second but then it almost turned into a high pitched shriek. That was the main thing that put me off to tell the truth. That and the fact he was cross-eyed. He'd be talking to you but looking away from you. Definitely weird!"

"What happened?"

"Nothing much, he bought me a drink in the Mason's Arms then said he wanted to come back to my place but I wouldn't do it. My sixth sense again."

"So what happened then?"

"Like I said, he wanted to come back to mine, I told him that I'd been feeling rough all day and thought I was coming down with something. He said that he could give me something to make me feel better back at my lodgings but I just weren't 'aving none of it, an' I told 'im so too! Y'know, polite but firm, if ya know what I mean? Anyhows, we said goodbye on Lambeth Bridge. Just before we parted he gave me a tablet from a little bottle in his pocket. He said, 'Take this now and you will feel much better in the morning'."

"And you took it?"

"Nah, of course I didn't! Like I said he was creepy so I palmed it, didn't I?"

"Palmed it?" repeated the detective.

Valerie broke in with a smirk "The oldest trick in the book, isn't it Louise?"

"Yeah of course it is. Have you got a ha'penny in your pocket, guv'nor?"

"Why?"

"Because I'm feeling a bit peckish. Give me the ha'penny so's I can eat it."

Randan handed her a ha'penny piece and watched her put the coin into her mouth and apparently swallow it."

Randan looked astonished. "But why would you do that?"

"Do what, guv'nor?"

"Why, swallow that coin of course!"

"Make a fist with your right hand, guv'nor."

Randan again did as she asked.

"Now open your fist, guv'nor."

As Randan opened his hand Louise reached forward, touched his palm and revealed the ha'penny coin "Do you mean this ha'penny, guv'nor? That's what I means by palming. Now don't tell me that you ain't never seen that trick done before? An' you a copper an' all! It's the oldest trick in the book, guv'nor! Anyhows, that's what I did to the Yank's tablet. Good trick, ain't it guv'nor?"

Randan gazed at Louise "Indeed it is a good trick, Miss Harvey. What is more, it is a trick which probably saved your life. We believe that tablet probably contained sufficient poison to kill you. I don't suppose that you kept the tablet, did you?"

"Nah, guv'nor. As soon as I palmed it, I dropped it in the river."

"You did very well, Louise. When we catch this man will you tell that story in court if you are asked to?"

"Will I 'ave to do the palming trick again?"

Randan smiled again. "No, I don't imagine so, Louise. But you will be punishing the man who murdered Ellen and Matilda."

"Yeah, I'll do it for them, guv'nor."

Chapter Fourteen

Having left Louise Harvey to rejoice in her good fortune, they all reconvened at New Scotland Yard.

Randan addressed the small group. "Thanks to Patrick's information we now know that Cream is back in London, and he has attacked another three women, killing two of them. We don't yet know what his intentions are and we have no idea how long he intends to stay here. What I think we can be certain of is that if we don't stop him now, he will almost certainly kill again. Furthermore, I think we can be sure that if we don't catch him and hold on to him this time, we may never get another chance. We have all the evidence we need to put him before a judge and jury so it is just a matter of arresting him. But we will only get one chance. Once he realises that the police know he is back, he will run and that could be the end of it. Does anyone have any suggestions?"

There were a few seconds of silence as the detective looked at all the group. Patrick O'Malley was the first to speak. "I know I have no authority here, sir and you have already been very generous in allowing me to be a part of this investigation. But I do have a suggestion, if you would like to hear it."

"Detective O'Malley, any suggestions that you have will most definitely be considered. You are the only person here who has seen Cream since his return to London. You have followed your instincts and so far they have been entirely correct, so please let us know your thoughts."

"It's really very simple, sir. My meeting with Cream happened purely by chance when my cousins and I were visiting his known and suspected haunts in Lambeth. My suggestion is that I try and find him again. When I parted from Cream after my tour, I decided to ask how I might be able to contact him again in the future without raising his suspicions of me. You will remember that I mentioned he was very eager to take me on his tour of the murder locations and that he wanted to charge me a lot more than the fairly modest amount that I managed to bargain him down to? I suggested to him that I might be able put together a larger group of my friends and relatives and that the group would be willing to pay him one pound each for one of his walks." O'Malley paused for a second. "From the smile on his face I could tell that the idea of more easy money was most attractive to him and indeed he joked that if that could be arranged then he would look upon that day's tour as an excellent investment. So I asked him how I might best be able to contact him if I could raise sufficient interest in another tour. I was hoping that he would give me an address but he just smiled and told me that he could usually be found in Gatti's Music Hall on a Friday night. Then he winked at me and said, 'You have seen that it has a ready supply of attractive ladies.'"

The group murmured their approval. "Thank you, Patrick, that sounds promising. Are you thinking of doing this alone?"

"Yes, sir, I think so. He seems to trust me but also he already knows you and Sergeant Parry from your original arrest so I can't be with either of you and although I was with my cousins in a group, he approached me when I was alone. I don't think I would be in any danger and of course we know already, he is greedy for money."

"Yes, I know that, but I don't like the idea of sending you looking for him alone."

Valerie interjected, "I have a suggestion too. Why don't I go with Detective O'Malley?"

All eyes turned to Randan. "No, Valerie, absolutely not! It's completely out of the question. Sir Edward would have my guts for garters if he knew about this and I don't imagine that your husband would be overly delighted with me agreeing to let you attend a meeting with a known murderer."

"Oh, come now, Peter. Patrick will be with me and as long as I don't accept any tablets from Cream, I should be quite safe."

Again Randan was firm. "No, Valerie, I won't allow it. In fact, I forbid it."

Valerie's eyes flashed with anger. "You forbid it? Who the devil do you think you are talking to, Inspector Randan? I am not an employee of the police, I am a free woman and I may go wherever I please and be in the company of whoever I wish. If Patrick and I wish to spend a night at Gatti's Music Hall together, it is absolutely none of your damn business!"

Valerie's anger brought about a stunned silence in the room which was broken by an even angrier response from Joan. "Lady Meux! How dare you address Inspector Randan in such a rude manner in his own office!" All eyes now turned in amazement towards Joan who was now in full flow. "Do you need reminding, Lady Meux, that the only reason Mr Randan accepted this case was in response to your own request? This is now a police investigation and Inspector Randan is in sole charge of it. You are here purely because of his courtesy to you. Of course he wants to catch this terrible man, but he is also responsible for the safety of everyone involved and that includes you and Detective O'Malley!"

There was another stunned silence, this time it was broken by Valerie now speaking in a hushed voice and with just the hint of a tear in her eye. "I'm sorry. I was forgetting myself, perhaps this matter has affected us all far more than we realise but that is no excuse for my previous outburst. Thank you, Joan, for reminding me of my manners and you are, of course absolutely correct. I apologise unreservedly to you all. Sometimes I forget that my current rank in society does not give me the right to behave like a spoilt child. Of course Peter must be in complete charge and I am deeply sorry for suggesting otherwise."

Randan was once again able to take command. "Thank you to both of you, but we must all keep our eyes focused on the job in hand and the plain truth is that I don't have a better plan than the idea suggested by Detective O'Malley. Valerie, what would be the reason for Patrick and you going to Gatti's?"

"The oldest reason known to man of course. Patrick would be showing a girl a good time. I may be a little older than Patrick but I will still look better than most of the working girls there!"

Randan looked genuinely shocked and Valerie smiled when she saw him blushing."

"Stop worrying, Peter. I will simply be playing a role, I will be 'treading the boards' just as I intended to do all those years ago and as you yourself said, 'We will only get one chance at this' and as you also just said, you don't have any better ideas!"

Randan was torn. "When are you thinking of trying this?"

Patrick replied "Friday night, sir. Today is Thursday, I suggest tomorrow night."

"I must have lost my mind," whispered Randan to himself. "Very well. At least we will have tomorrow to consider our options, but if we do go ahead with Patrick's plan tomorrow night, I want it to be clearly understood that your aim will be to make contact with Cream or Harrison as he seems to be calling himself this time, and to make an appointment to bring him out into the open where we can arrest him with a minimum of fuss. The last thing we want to do is to start a mass Friday night brawl in Gatti's which is highly likely if we attempt to arrest him there. Are we all agreed?"

The group was once again smiling at each other as they all nodded their agreement.

At six the following Friday evening, Detective Patrick O'Malley and Lady Valerie Meux met in Inspector Randan's office at New Scotland Yard.

"Are you two both ready for tonight?"

"I think so, sir," replied the New Yorker.

"Very well, I am not going to labour the point but you both know what I want you to do. Your job is to try and make contact with Cream, suggest that you have a group to go on one of his tours and get him to agree to a meet in a public place where we can safely arrest him on our own terms. Please be careful and sensible. Remember this man is a killer and you are under no circumstances to put yourselves at risk."

Valerie and Patrick nodded their agreement, left New Scotland Yard and then hailed a hansom cab on the Victoria Embankment to convey them Gatti's Music Hall.

"Are you nervous, Lady Meux? queried the American detective.

Valerie smiled back at him. "Not really, Patrick, a little excited perhaps, but not really nervous. Peter has given us firm instructions and I intend to stick to them as rigidly as possible. By the way, since we are 'under cover', is that the correct term for this type of work? I think we should get into character. You must call me Val from now on and I will only call you Pat. We met for the first time this afternoon and you are taking me for an evening's entertainment at the music hall. It's a nice simple story for us to stick to."

The detective smiled. "You are absolutely right Val. The simpler the cover story, the easier it is to stick to."

Just before they left the cab Valerie slipped Patrick a few coins to pay the fare which he did before they both entered the music hall by the main entrance. Gatti's was still fairly quiet but was just beginning to fill up with customers eagerly awaiting their evening of entertainment. Patrick made for the area where he had been standing when he had first met Cream. He selected a table and pulled the chair out for Val to sit on before sitting down himself.

"Any sign of him, Pat?"

Pat shook his head "It's a little early yet. It was about eight thirty when I saw him last time. Let me get us a drink."

Patrick made his way to the bar and returned with a glass of wine for Val and a glass of pale ale for himself. "Let's hope he is not too long. The fuller this place gets the more difficult it will be to spot him."

Val reached across the table and clinked Pat's glass in a flirtatious manner "Cheers, Pat. Look happy, you are supposed to be enjoying yourself."

"Have you ever been to a place like this before, Val?"

Val smiled back, "Yes, I have Pat and it seems like a lifetime ago. But I think I can remember the basics."

The pair sat quietly sipping their drinks and just as the clock showed eight, Pat spotted Cream standing near the bar by a column. "He's here, Val, he's standing behind you but don't turn around."

Val fought against the instinct to turn around to get her first glimpse of the murderer. "Are you going to approach him, Pat?"

"No, not yet, the venue is still fairly quiet so I'll see if he spots me. I think it will be better if he makes the first move,"

Cream was standing by the column near the bar and was carefully looking around the slowly filling hall. After a few seconds, his eyes rested on the table where Pat and Val were seated, he smiled and walked slowly towards them. "Good evening, Patrick. This is a most unexpected surprise. Are you here tonight with your family again?"

Patrick rose to meet Cream and offered him his hand. "Good evening, Mr. Harrison. No, sir, no cousins tonight. I'm here with my friend Val. I asked her if she would care to accompany me to the music hall tonight and she has very graciously accepted my offer."

Val smiled at the newcomer but could feel his eyes undressing her as she bade him good evening. For a few moments her mind was taken back to the nights when she worked at the Casino de Venice in Holborn all those years ago and the way this man was looking at her sent a shiver down her spine.

Cream was smartly dressed in formal evening wear with a top hat and monocle. He removed his top hat and studied

Val with great interest. "Well Patrick, you are to be hugely congratulated in securing the company of this most exquisite creature. I am extremely jealous of your good fortune."

Val had to fight the urge to toss her glass of wine into Cream's face for his obnoxious misogyny but instead smiled sweetly back at him. "Won't you join us, sir? Pat, why don't you go to the bar, sweetheart, and get Mr Harrison a drink. It's not often that one gets the chance to meet a real gentleman! May I ask what your profession is, sir?

Cream could not contain his enthusiasm and his face broke into a broad smile. "I would be delighted to join you, Val and I'm actually a physician." Turning to Pat he said, "Get me a brandy will you, please, Patrick?"

Pat made to move towards the bar which was beginning to get busy. "I was hoping to meet you again, Mr Harrison. When I come back, I would like to discuss a business matter with you. I think I have about ten people who would very much like to go on one of your Lambeth Murder walks and are happy to pay you ten pounds for your time."

Cream could barely take his eyes off Val. "Really, Patrick? That sounds absolutely fascinating. Now run along and get that drink, will you? There's a good chap. This bar is getting quite full now so you will probably save time by going to the smaller bar around the back."

O'Malley did not like the idea of leaving Valerie alone with Cream and was determined to return as quickly as possible.

No sooner had he disappeared from view than Cream moved his chair next to Val's and reached across to take her hand. The smile on his face was more like a leer. "Young O'Malley really does display excellent taste in his choice of female company, Val, and it does seem rather a shame that we must disappoint him. But, as the saying goes 'Two's company and three is a crowd'. Let us retire to somewhere where we can be alone. I really do think that you will find my professional company far more to your liking than that of our young friend from New York!"

Valerie maintained her smile and said "Now, sir, that

does not sound like a very gentlemanly way to treat Patrick and I'm sure I don't know what he has done to deserve such ill treatment from you. Besides, he is bringing you a brandy so what's your hurry?"

Cream held her hand in a slightly tighter grip. "You misunderstand me, Val, O'Malley has done nothing to upset or annoy me. Indeed, I fully intend to take him up on that offer of taking his group on one of my 'Murder tours'. But that can wait. I fully intend to have the pleasure of you all to myself tonight. I will give you experiences that you could never even dream of and I am sure that Patrick will forgive me this one tiny deceit against him. Now, quickly, let us depart before he returns. Come with me."

Val refused to budge and the smile had now left her face. "I am going nowhere alone with you, sir, and that's the end of it!"

As soon as she had spoken, Cream's smile changed to a snarl. "Oh Val, you disappoint me. I had hoped that you would be amenable to my plan for tonight. But I am afraid that I must insist. You will be coming with me, right now!"

Val flinched as she felt a sharp, pointed blade pressing into the flesh just below her ribs. "What on earth are you doing, Mr Harrison?"

"You will find out soon enough my dear. Do as I say and I promise that no harm will befall you. Now, get to your feet."

Cream guided Val towards the nearest exit. At a table in front of them sat two burly workmen slumped over the table and clearly the worse for drink. Cream brushed against the larger of the two men who reacted with displeasure and slurred "Who do ya think you're pushing, matey?"

Cream tried to push past him and shouted, "Get out of my way, you drunken fool!"

The large man rose to his feet and spun Cream around. "Drunken fool, am I?"

Cream waved the blade at his attacker who grabbed his hand and forced it onto the bar table before smashing a heavy pint glass tankard across the back of his hand forcing him to drop the blade. Before Cream could scream in agony, he was felled by a crisp left hook from the workman who was proving to be remarkably agile for a drunk.

"Oh, thank you so much, gentlemen. I think you may just have saved my life!

The burly workman turned and faced Val for the first time "That's quite alright, Val. We are only too pleased to help!"

Val gasped in amazement "Peter! Nathan! What are you two doing here?"

Randan was now grinning. "You didn't really imagine that we would let you come here without any protection at all, did you? We had to keep an eye on you just in case things didn't go according to plan."

"Just as well we did," added Nathan.

Seconds later O'Malley joined them "What the hell happened?"

Val looked at him and said, "It seems that Dr. Cream had not read our script, Patrick."

O'Malley looked at his glass of brandy. "What about this?"

Randan took it from his hand. "It seems a shame to waste it," and downed the glass in one. "Now, let's get our friend here to the police station." Randan seized his prisoner's right arm and twisted it behind his back. This time he would be marched the short distance to Lambeth Police Station without the option of accompanying them willingly. Cream attempted to struggle free, but the detective just applied the hammerlock even tighter on his bent right arm causing Cream to gasp in pain.

The arrival of Randan's group at the police station caused something of a stir. Cream had recovered his composure by the time he was seated in the charge room. Randan had rather expected him to start making a fuss upon his arrival, but Cream maintained a sullen silence during the initial procedures. Patrick and Valerie were directed to a side office and asked to wait there.

The duty officer was summoned and listened carefully to

Randan's explanation as to why and how Cream had been arrested. Having satisfied himself that all was as it should be he asked Sergeant Parry and the station officer to begin the required paperwork. "Can I have a word with you in private, please Inspector Randan?"

Randan nodded and followed the duty Inspector into his small office just off the station's front office where Patrick and Val were seated. As the door was closed behind them the duty inspector smiled and offered Randan his hand. "Congratulations Inspector Randan, I must admit I didn't think we would see this man back in police custody, but you have proved me wrong. Do I gather that this lady and gentleman are also involved in the arrest?"

Randan returned his smile. "Thank you, and, yes. This is Lady Valerie Meux whose information initiated this whole investigation, and this is Detective Patrick O'Malley from the New York Police Department whose assistance has proved invaluable."

The duty officer shook them both warmly by the hand. "Inspector Randan, is there any need to detain Lady Meux and Detective O'Malley any further? I suggest one of my men secures a hansom cab to take them wherever they need to go. You can take any statements that you need from them another time."

Randan agreed and Valerie and Patrick were quite happy to let Randan and Parry handle the more mundane aspects of police work. The cab was summoned to take them back to New Scotland Yard.

Once they had departed, Randan spoke again to the duty inspector "I must admit that I had my doubts as to whether I would ever see him stand trial, but it looks as if our hard work will prove worthwhile. Though I don't mind telling you that good fortune has smiled upon us on various occasions during this investigation."

"I firmly believe that we make our own luck, and you fully deserve any good fortune that may have come your way. Some of your methods may have been, may I say, unorthodox? But ultimately you will be responsible for removing a dangerous and callous murderer from our streets."

"Let's not get too far ahead of ourselves," cautioned Randan. "He may be in custody, but we must remember what a cunning and devious man Cream is. I want him watched and fully supervised for the entire time he is in police custody. I don't want him pulling any of the tricks that we know he has up his sleeve."

"I'm already ahead of you there, Inspector. I will suggest to the superintendent that he is physically restrained whilst in our custody and one officer is to be in his cell with him at all times with another officer within earshot in case of unforeseen problems."

"Will your superintendent agree to that use of manpower?"

"Oh, yes, without doubt. The last thing he wants is for him to be in any way involved with another escaping prisoner. You leave that part to me. Just one thing, are you going to interview him to see if he will confess?"

Randan considered the idea for a few seconds. "Yes, I think Sergeant Parry and myself will interview him, although I really don't expect him to admit any guilt whatsoever. I rather think he will fight this all to the bitter end. But we shall see. Let's complete the paperwork and get him locked up overnight. Then we can interview him and get him charged tomorrow."

"Speaking of the charges," queried the uniformed inspector. "What do you anticipate the charges to be?"

"Four charges of murder plus an additional charge of attempted murder against Louise Harvey, She was fortunate enough to be suspicious of his motives and palmed the tablet of strychnine instead of swallowing it. I expect the prosecution also to involve allegations of attempted extortion."

"Louise Harvey must consider herself a very lucky lady. I don't suppose she kept the tablet, did she?"

Randan grinned. "No, unfortunately not. That would have been the icing on our cake! She threw it into the river.

But her evidence and identification of Cream will undoubtedly be vital to the prosecution's evidence."

The two inspectors returned to the charge room as the station officer and Parry were completing listing the prisoner's property. The station officer read over the list and offered Cream the opportunity to countersign the list below his own signature, but Cream just stared blankly ahead and the station officer simply added the words 'prisoner refused to sign'.

The duty officer addressed Cream directly "Thomas Neill Cream. You have been arrested on a warrant for murder. You will now be held here overnight, and the investigation will continue tomorrow. Do you understand?"

Cream spoke for the first time since he had arrived in the charge room. "If you have sufficient evidence to charge me with any offences, which, by the way, I completely deny and refute. Why don't you just charge me now and get this farce over with? The sooner I can stand before a judge and jury, the quicker I can prove my absolute innocence as regards these ludicrous insinuations."

The inspector looked up from his paperwork, adjusted his spectacles and calmly replied, "All in good time Doctor, all in good time. Now, go with these officers to the cells." And then turning to the constables said, "Gentlemen. Do not let him out of your sight for even a second.

Cream was then led away to the cells and Randan and Parry heard the cell passage door slam securely behind him.

"Don't worry, gentlemen" said the duty inspector to Randan and Parry. "We will look after him well and you can interview him tomorrow."

Randan and Parry thanked the Lambeth officers, left the station at around eleven thirty and headed back across the Thames to meet up with Valerie and O'Malley who had been joined by Joan in the Criminal Records Office where they had been eagerly awaiting their arrival.

Randan and Parry related their story with great relish. Joan smiled to herself as she hadn't seen Randan so happy and excited since beginning the investigation.

When all the gaps had been filled in, Valerie added her thanks and congratulations. "One thing, Peter. We should inform Sir Edward that the arrest has been made. I know this is your case, but I would rather like to be with you when you do tell him officially. Will that be all right?"

The detective smiled across at her. "Valerie, if it had not been for your work and intervention on behalf of the vulnerable women of Lambeth, there would have been no investigation, no arrest and possibly Cream would still be at large murdering women with complete impunity. Therefore it is absolutely right and proper for you to be present when Sir Edward is officially informed. I suggest that we meet here first thing tomorrow morning and that all five of us go up and give Sir Edward the good news. I am absolutely positive he will welcome some good news in this case at long last. Having done that, Nathan and I will go and interview our suspect and I think this time we can leave Sir Edward to conduct his own press interview."

The following morning saw Randan, Valerie, Parry, Joan and O'Malley standing in the Commissioner's office in New Scotland Yard in front of a positively beaming Sir Edward Bradford. "Well done, indeed to all of you and particularly you, Randan. I can't say that there were not times when I doubted if you were the right man for the job, but you proved me wrong in the end."

"Thank you, Sir Edward but our task is not completed yet and won't be until Cream is convicted at the Old Bailey," replied Randan.

"Surely that is just a formality, isn't it? Don't tell me that you have doubts about the strength of the evidence in your case?"

"Certainly not sir. The case is solid and I am confident of gaining a conviction, it's just that you can never be truly sure of an outcome at court until the jury pronounces the accused 'Guilty'."

"Do we have any idea when the trial might be?"

"Not yet, sir. I don't believe that the case can be committed to the Old Bailey until the inquests for the deceased women have been completed. That may delay the final trial somewhat."

"I see; is there anything else to do in the meantime?"

"Not really, sir. Sergeant Parry and I will attend Lambeth Police Station when we are finished here, and we will interview Cream, but I don't expect him to confess his crimes. Indeed, he may refuse to say anything at all."

"I'm glad you are so confident. I have a press conference that will take place while you will be interviewing Cream. It will be good to be able to give them some good news at last."

"Do they really want 'good news', sir?"

"Probably not, Randan. 'Excellent work done by the police' does not sell papers. 'Inefficient and incompetent police blunder again' *does* sell papers unfortunately. One thing before you go to Lambeth though. Detective O'Malley here. How important is his evidence to your case? It may be difficult to get him back from the United States if he goes back home before the trial."

Randan replied, knowing that once again he was ahead of the Commissioner.

"The required arrangements have already been made via the American Embassy, Sir Edward. Detective O'Malley's assistance has been invaluable in resolving this case and his evidence will be required at the trial. With that in mind, I have already arranged for him to remain on official secondment, attached to the Metropolitan Police until the trial has finished. His senior officers are very happy to allow him to remain working with us, which will they think add greatly to his policing experiences."

"Excellent. I shall let you and Parry get on with your interview and I will go and meet the press. Good luck, Randan, and well done again to all of you."

The small group filed out of the office and Randan and Parry headed across the Thames to Lambeth. Meanwhile, Valerie suggested to the others that now would be the ideal time to pay one more visit to the Savoy Grill for refreshments. Joan and Detective O'Malley needed no second invitation to join her.

An hour later, Randan and Parry were sitting behind a desk in Lambeth Police Station awaiting the arrival of Doctor Cream. The door opened and Cream was led handcuffed and shackled into the room before being pushed onto a seat opposite the two detectives.

Cream managed a surly smile. "I was wondering how long it would be before you came back to gloat over me. Inspector Randan, isn't it?"

Randan finished writing in his notebook for a few seconds before raising his head and looking at Cream. "Yes, that is correct, Dr Cream. I am Inspector Randan and this is Sergeant Parry. Very shortly you will be charged. The charges will be several counts of murder, and various other offences that relate to extortion. Tomorrow you will appear at the local police court where you will be remanded in custody until your trial at the Central Criminal Court. This represents your last opportunity to address us before your trial."

Cream smiled through his gritted teeth. "Do you really expect me to do your job for you and confess all my sins to you before my trial, Inspector?"

Randan stared coldly into Cream's eyes. "You mistake me for a priest, sir. I have absolutely no interest in hearing you confess your sins and I am certainly not qualified to absolve you of them. I am far more interested in seeing you convicted of murder and then watching as you leave this world to explain yourself in the next. Perhaps God may forgive you, but I never will."

Cream's smile vanished. "I tire of this banter, Inspector but I must say that you fascinate me on a professional level. I have underestimated your abilities and that is why I find myself in this unfortunate and undeserved position. Let me make this completely clear. I admit absolutely nothing and I maintain my innocence to whatever your charges might be. However, I wish to talk to you alone, man to man, and perhaps we might better understand one another."

Parry looked across at his senior officer. "I would advise against it, sir. We already know how devious this man can be.

Even if he says anything it will remain inadmissible in evidence without a witness to corroborate what was said."

Randan closed his eyes for a second. "Thank you, Sergeant Parry. Please leave us but remain immediately outside the door. If I need you, I will call you and the prisoner is in no position to move swiftly."

Parry nodded and exited the room, closing the door behind him. As soon as the door was closed, Randan looked intently at his prisoner. "What do you want, Cream?"

"Simply for us both to have a better understanding of each other, Inspector. Let us imagine, for a second, simply for amusement, that I really am guilty of the terrible crimes that you imagine I may have committed. Why do you imagine that I, a professional man committed by oath to saving lives, should actually resort to taking lives instead? "

Randan replied quietly, "I really have no idea. But you would not be the first person to gain pleasure from killing and I doubt you will be the last. And, by the way, I know of the crimes you committed in America."

Cream's voice rose to a shrill pitch. "Oh dear, I see your American assistant has been very busy. But I am sure you realise that those allegations will be inadmissible in evidence against me in a British court. They were, of course, entirely false allegations and even if they were true, you can't use them in evidence. You do realise that, Inspector, don't you?"

Randan remained poker-faced "Of course I do. Our evidence is based solely on the crimes you have committed in London since you arrived last year."

"Very sensible, Inspector. But still we have not arrived at why I might choose to commit such diabolical acts. Doesn't it interest you, Inspector Randan?"

Randan allowed a slight smile to play on his lips. "Well Doctor, since we are dealing purely in hypothetical matters, why don't you tell me why you think any man might commit such acts, in your professional opinion, of course."

"I believe, Inspector, that your *real* suspect might possibly be someone with a point to prove, albeit a rather dark and morbid point. It *may* be that your true killer might be someone who has viewed recent criminal events in London's history and thought to himself, I can do better than that!"

Randan became serious. "Are you referring to the Whitechapel Murders?"

"That would certainly be a fair comparison, Inspector. Clumsy and overly violent murders designed to grab the public's attention and, of course, that of the press. Committed, I believe, by a psychopathic attention seeker. I think your true suspect is perhaps trying to outdo the man known as 'Jack the Ripper'. But your suspect is infinitely superior in intellect and ability and, of course, he is absolutely more subtle and refined than the thuggish butcher who committed the Whitechapel Murders."

Randan looked at Cream with a quizzical expression on his face. "You think my suspect was trying to compete in some way with the Whitechapel murderer?"

"Yes, I think that is possibly the case and he has already succeeded in equalling the Ripper's body count. Both have killed five times. But your suspect has done so without raising the hue and cry and could possibly continue his work unhindered with the world being unaware that anything is amiss, because of the nature of his victims and because of the true murderer's cleverness and ability to avoid detection and capture as he goes about his work."

"So, you believe that my true suspect is competing against the Whitechapel Murderer to achieve some sort of eternal notoriety?"

Cream nodded. "Very possibly, yes."

"I am afraid that I can't agree with you, Doctor. Also, I doubt your arithmetic. The Whitechapel Murderer was credited with five victims. But my suspect for these murders in Lambeth has only killed on four occasions."

"Really, Inspector? Perhaps I was correct in my original opinion of you. I do know quite a lot about these murders and your murderer has killed five women. I can even name them for you, Donworth, Clover, Harvey, Marsh and Shrivel."

"Doctor Cream, I am afraid it is your arithmetic that is awry here. The Lambeth Poisoner has only killed four women. The fifth victim that you mentioned, Louise Harvey, is alive and well. You see, Doctor, she was suspicious of you from the moment she met you and when you gave her the strychnine pill on Lambeth Bridge, she only pretended to swallow it. Then she threw it harmlessly in the river. You will be charged with just four counts of murder and one count of the attempted murder of Louise Harvey and it will be her evidence of identification that will see you hang at Newgate Prison!"

Cream's voice rose to almost a scream. "No! I don't believe you. You are lying!"

"No, Doctor. I am telling you the truth. You have only killed four women. Your name will never be famous. Dr. Thomas Neill Cream will just become a minor footnote in criminal history. Are you still out there, Sergeant Parry?"

Parry opened the door "I am, sir."

"Good. Summon the goaler please, let's get this prisoner formally charged."

Cream was charged exactly as Randan had told him with the murders of Ellen Donworth, Matilda Clover, Alice Marsh and Emma Shrivel and the attempted murder of Louise Harvey. In addition, he was also charged with three other counts of attempted extortion.

Thomas Cream's trial at the Old Bailey lasted from 17th to the 21st of October and a guilty verdict was never really in doubt. Indeed, the jury took just twelve minutes to return a verdict of guilty on all charges.

On the morning of Tuesday, 15th November 1892, Inspector Peter Randan and Sergeant Nathaniel Parry were escorted to the execution cell of Newgate Prison by the prison governor. Before they entered the cell, Randan whispered to Parry. "Nathan, you really don't have to come in and watch this, I can do this alone."

Parry attempted to smile but instead just managed a swallow. "Thank you, sir. It's all right. We have come this far so we should see this through together."

Randan simply nodded and they both entered the execution cell and took their places by the governor's side. In front of them, they could see the rope hanging above the trap door from a stout supporting beam that was secured some nine feet above the floor. Randan judged the rope to be about six feet in length.

When he was led into the execution cell, Cream presented a pathetic and terrified figure. Before him walked the prison Ordinary. Cream's hands had already been secured behind his back before being taken to meet his end, having already angrily refused to confess his sins. The executioner, James Billington, slipped a hood over Cream's head and led him blindly forward. The witnesses could hear Cream whimpering softly as Billington edged him forward, slipped the rope over his head and around his neck before carefully adjusting and tightening the noose. Cream now stood still and silent but a fraction of a second before Billington pulled the lever to open the trap door he began to shout in his shrill and squeaky voice. As he dropped through the trapdoor into oblivion he yelled "I'M JACK THE RI……….."

Parry turned to Randan. "Did you hear that, sir?"

Randan replied, "No Sergeant. I didn't hear a thing." He then turned and walked silently and slowly from the cell.

On Friday November 18th all of those involved in the case were invited to assemble in Sir Edward Bradford's private office at New Scotland Yard. Valerie looked magnificent in a dress that could only have been made in Paris.

Randan had a broad grin on his face. "You look wonderful, Valerie."

Valerie smiled in pleasure at the compliment. "Why thank you, Peter. You look very smart yourself. And it is entirely right that we should make the effort. This is a day that I had feared we would never reach, and you and your team are entirely responsible for seeing that justice has been finally done. I am also sure that Teddy will acknowledge that in his speech."

"May I ask how you can be so sure, Valerie?"

"Because I wrote most of his speech for him, of course!"

Randan laughed out loud. "I may have said this before, Lady Meux. But you really are a most remarkable woman!"

Commissioner Bradford's actual address went on rather longer than perhaps even Valerie had intended, but he did include the important items that she had inserted. "For their dedication to duty in solving this difficult and complex case the two officers, Inspector Peter Randan and Sergeant Nathaniel Parry would both receive promotions to the ranks of Chief Inspector and Inspector, respectively. Detective O'Malley from the New York Police Department will be awarded a special citation recognising the part that he played in the investigation and I understand that he will also be promoted upon his return to the United States. This leaves just one other person involved who I have not yet mentioned, namely, Chief inspector Randan's civilian assistant, Mrs Joan Merriweather. For you, Joan, I have been persuaded to award something that I understand will help you in your future work with Chief Inspector Randan. I am giving you this typewriter. I may not like the blessed things myself, but I have been convinced that perhaps they should play a part in the future of policing the Metropolis."

Joan had probably never grinned so broadly as when she removed the cover from her brand-new machine, which Nathan gallantly volunteered to carry down to the Criminal Records Office three floors below.

Following Sir Edward's reception, Valerie led Randan into a quiet corner. "Peter, when this is all over will you join me at the Savoy Grill? There is something that I would like to say to you in private, if you don't mind."

Randan smiled. "Of course, Valerie. We can walk there together. I think Sir Edward's reception is just about finished now, anyway."

"No Peter, I think we should both go there separately. I really don't want to risk the press seeing us arrive together."

Randan looked a little puzzled but agreed to her request.

A few minutes later Valerie made a big show of saying her goodbyes to Sir Edward and of leaving the reception. A few minutes after that, Randan made his way to the Criminal Records Office and told Nathan and Joan that he needed to leave a little early and that he would see them both the following day. He then walked the short distance along the Victoria Embankment to the Savoy Grill. As he entered through the River Terrace entrance, he was greeted by the smiling figure of Joseph who took him to Valerie's private booth.

"Thank you for coming Peter and I'm sorry to be so melodramatic but I have a couple of things to say to you and I want to say them to you in private."

"There is no need to say anything, Valerie. This has been an adventure that I would not have missed for the world. In getting together again after all these years we have managed to rid London of a dangerous killer. Also, if you had not sought me out to assist you and Rose, then I might have been stuck in the Criminal Records Office for the rest of my service. It really is me who should be thanking you!"

"You really are the sweetest of men, Peter. I just wanted you to know the full depth of my appreciation for what you have done for me personally. Not least for when you very probably saved my life – again – in Gatti's Music Hall when you arrested that awful man."

Randan grinned at her. "I could hardly let him do away with my chief witness and crime fighting partner, could I?"

"No, I suppose not," replied Valerie. "But you know Peter, 'Crime fighting partners' has a certain ring to it, don't you think? Perhaps if Rose and I were to come across other nefarious, criminal activities during the course of our work, might I be allowed to seek you out again now that you will be a chief inspector?"

Randan's grin became wider. "Who can tell what the future might hold for either of us, Valerie?"

At that moment Joseph appeared beside them as if out of nowhere, "My apologies for interrupting, Lady Meux, but your transport has arrived."

Valerie smiled and stood up. "Peter, may I offer you a lift anywhere?"

"I was heading to the underground station, Valerie but if you are going eastwards perhaps you could drop me off at Blackfriars? Will that be taking you out of your way?"

Valerie flashed her most radiant smile at him. "Of course not, Peter. Blackfriars it shall be".

As they left the Savoy by the River Terrace door, Randan saw that their transport was a light carriage driven by Mary Gee and pulled by two zebras. "Jacob and Joshua, if I am not mistaken." said Randan.

The zebra carriage took less than fifteen minutes to reach Blackfriars. It would probably have been quicker but for the fact that amazed Londoners approached it wanting to stroke the zebras every time they drew to a halt on the Victoria Embankment.

At Blackfriars, Randan stepped down from the carriage and waved to Valerie as the carriage resumed its journey. He watched until the carriage disappeared around the bend in Farringdon Street, then checked his pocket watch and entered the station. As he stood on the platform, he wondered what challenges the future might bring. One thing seemed certain; his days of updating files in the Criminal Record Office at New Scotland Yard would soon be left far behind him.

Afterword

The inspiration for writing this story came to me whilst I was indulging in one of my favourite pastimes, reading old and interesting books about my home city of London. The book was entitled *London Town*, written by J.B. Booth and published by T. Werner Laurie in 1929. The book is simply a collection of stories and memories that had amused or entertained the author and two of his tales struck me as being of particular interest.

In the chapter titled 'Gaiety Girls and Matinee Idols' the author introduces his readers to Val Langdon. Young Val was born and grew up in Devon and decided to head to the bright lights of London. Once settled in London she found employment working as a banjo-playing barmaid and part time prostitute in the Casino de Venice, Holborn. It was there that she probably met her future husband third Baronet Henry Bruce Meux of Theobalds Park, heir to a brewing empire and one of the richest men in the country. Unsurprisingly, Val was never accepted into 'Polite Society' but this did not stop her from taking great delight in scandalising the upper classes whenever the opportunity presented itself. In the story I mention her riding around London in a carriage pulled by zebras, buying Temple Bar from the City of London Corporation and re-erecting it as a gatehouse to her estate in Theobalds Park, Cheshunt and commissioning a bankrupt James Whistler to paint her likeness in three separate portraits. This ended with her making a thinly-veiled threat against the artist after he made an inappropriate remark about her. I also mention her enthusiasm for ancient history. She became a noted Egyptologist and built up a fine collection of artefacts from that ancient era. All of these things actually happened (although probably not as I have described them). She would go on to own a Derby winning racehorse, 'Volodyovski' but this part of her life occurred later than the era of my tale and so does not feature in my story. Safe to say that Lady Valerie Meux, nee Val Langdon, was quite a character.

Later in Booth's book, in the chapter titled 'Press and Pressmen' he tells us about an unsavoury character named Thomas Neill Cream, a Scottish born doctor who returned to the United Kingdom via Canada and the United States where he was responsible for the deaths of several people to whom he administered strychnine. When he arrived in London via Liverpool, he continued his murderous ways by killing at least four women and attempting to kill a fifth in the area of Lambeth. These acts earned him the title of 'The Lambeth Poisoner'. Once again, the basic story of Thomas Cream is real, as are the names of his victims, Ellen Donworth, Matilda Clover, Alice Marsh and Emma Shrivel. Louise Harvey really did escape being murdered by 'palming' the tablet containing strychnine given to her by Cream and dropping it into the Thames.

So, there we have the ideas for my basic story. Having read Booth's book, I realised that the stories involving Lady Valerie Meux and Thomas Neill Cream both occurred contemporaneously. There is no evidence whatsoever to suggest that Valerie Meux cooperated with the Metropolitan Police in catching and convicting Cream, but it did seem to me that this was a fictitious story just begging to be written. 'Beautiful, and fabulously wealthy socialite with a somewhat colourful history, teams up with a New Scotland Yard detective to catch a devious and probably insane poisoner.'

Detective Inspector Peter Randan, his faithful assistant Joan Merriwether and Sergeant Nathan Parry are all purely fictitious. However, Sir Edward Bradford, The Commissioner of the Metropolitan Police at that time did exist. He was appointed in 1890 at a time when 'The Met' was coming under severe pressure after his three predecessors all left in quick succession following the Whitechapel Murders (1888). Bradford was previously an experienced military officer and he proved himself an able leader of the force. He remained in post until 1893. He was a keen huntsman and therefore it is not too much of a stretch of one's imagination to imagine him being invited to Henry and Valerie's Scottish hunting lodge. What drew me to give him such a prominent role in this story, however, was the fact that he really did have an extreme aversion to typewriters and telephones. He simply had to be included.

Another character who features on several occasions in the story, is Monsieur Joseph, the Maitre d'hotel at the Savoy Grill. Once again he was a real character and during the early years of the Savoy Grill, he became something of a legend in his own right. The Savoy customers at that time would have been mostly rich and powerful men and therefore Lady Valerie probably would not have had a private booth at that time. But why let the truth get in the way of a good story?

So my tale is a complete fiction based on some real events and containing some people who did really exist along with others who came entirely from my imagination. This brings me to the conclusion of my story, the capture, trial and final execution of Cream. It would seem that when Cream returned to London following his short time back in America, he did indeed meet an unnamed American police officer with whom he discussed at great length some of the murders. Cream's in-depth knowledge of the murders struck the officer as highly suspicious and it was he who alerted the Met. Police with regard to his suspicions that Dr. Cream was considerably more involved with the murders than he was letting on. He inspired the character of Patrick O'Malley who ultimately played such a pivotal role in my story.

Finally, several sources provide us with interesting

snippets of information regarding Cream himself. He was described as being handsome but also as having a noticeable squint and a very unusual voice that would rise almost to a shriek when he became excited. It would seem that he always dressed very smartly, and contemporary images depict him wearing a top hat and a monocle. Perhaps the most unusual description of Cream describes his final utterance at the moment of his execution. As he dropped through the trap door it was reported that he shouted, "I am Jack the……." It is a truly wonderful way to end his story. Unfortunately, that may too be a fiction. His executioner, James Billington reported these words as being his last. However, nobody else present at the execution corroborated his account and if those were indeed his last words as he left this world, you would really expect more than one eye witness to mention the fact. Having said that, of course. It is far too good a fiction for a budding new author to leave out of his tale.

One other interesting footnote. On a recent visit to New Scotland Yard's world-renowned Crime Museum, I came face to face with Cream's leather medicine case which still contains the glass containers in which he would have kept the chemicals that he used to commit his murders. So Randan was actually wrong in the final chapter. Dr. Thomas Neill Cream really did achieve a degree of historical fame and notoriety as 'The Lambeth Poisoner'.

Printed in Great Britain
by Amazon